NINJA DEATH VOW

Katsumi Toda

Published by

dragon books

**"BEHOLD, DEATH IS MY VOW,
COLD AS ICE!"**
(from the secret scrolls of the Tomokatsu Ryu)

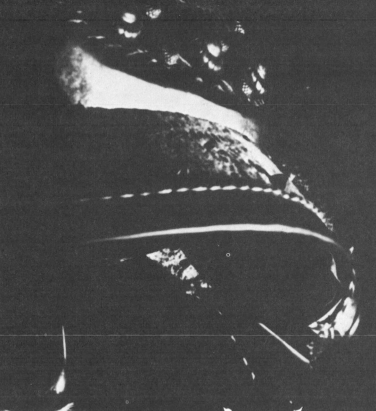

ninja death vow

acknowledgements

David Chambers/Publisher
Lesley Anne Copp-Taylor/Editor
Malcolm Copp-Taylor/Line drawings & photography
Island Design/Layout & design
Haruko Chambers/Special Translation

Library of Congress Catalogue Card No. 85.50038
ISBN 0 946062 110

Printed by Anchor Brendon Ltd
Tiptree, Essex, United Kingdom
First Published October 1985
Second impression March 1986

U.S. Distributor
Sakura Dragon Corporation

contents

The black ships at Uraga

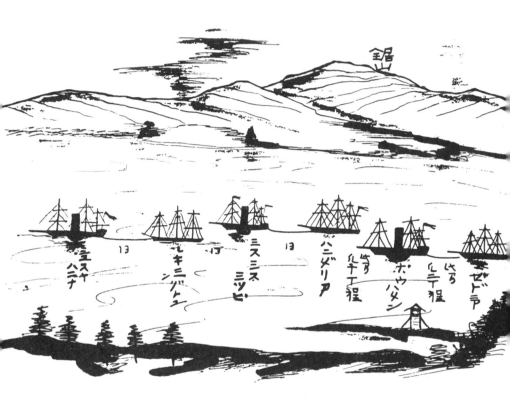

the black ship

The metal-clad bow of the steam frigate, "Mississippi", ploughed through the dark waters of Uraga Bay, spewing white foam. In her wake followed five similar vessels, hanging proudly from her masthead was the stars and stripes of "Old Glory".

The order was given and the sails were drawn in. The great steam engine pulsed slower; with a rattle and a whine, the great anchor chain snaked down into the foaming waters; the "Mississippi" came to rest. High upon the main deck, a lone watch sailor cast his telescope across the horizon in a lazy arc. He focused the brass and leather tube and a waving forest of pine trees came sharply into view. No pine trees these – twenty deep they lined the coastline. Clad in full battle armour and bearing the long Yari spears, bedecked with lacquered scabbards, edged with bear-skin, tigerskin and the long tail-feathers of prize fighting cocks. The lone watch reeled back at his first sight of the awesome Samurai.

From behind him came a mountain of a man, dressed in the uniform of bo'sun. At his side was the short cutlass, which together with his silver pipe, was the badge of his office.

He stroked his mutton-chop whiskers for a second, in an almost contemplative mood, then reached for the telescope.

"Seen the Japanners eh? Let's have me a squint. Can't be too different from a Chinee."

The watch, his eyes glazed, his mouth slightly open, handed over his telescope.

"Now then, what have we here my hearties" the bo'sun muttered as he put the glass to his eye.

He scanned back and forth across the horizon, spat a long stream of red tobacco juice over the side of the ship and jamming

Kari Mata whistling arrow

the telescope closer to his eye gasped,
"Lord God A' Mighty; old Bruin oughta see this". He was almost
thinking out loud.

"Better let old Bruin see then" boomed a deep bass voice.

The bo'sun jumped to attention and turned around to salute –
no mean feat for a man of 220lbs. His salute was crisply returned
by a man in Commodore's uniform. He was a tall hulk of a man,
with a heart as big as his home state, his stern face was creased
slightly in a wry smile.

"At ease pipes" said Commodore Matthew C. Perry. He
reached for the telescope.

"Well they certainly are a fierce looking crew, but we'll see
what a bit of American grit can do."

On the shore, rank upon rank of Samurai waited; watching.
Not since the fall of Osaka Castle, over two hundred and thirty
years ago, had such an army gathered in earnest. Hands gloved in
stencilled leather gripped the fine lacquer of scabbards bearing
brave blades that had not seen action since that time. The spirits
of long dead warriors rose up and stalked the land. High above the
first rank of twenty deep sat Ikeda Mitsunari, the personal
emissary of Tokugawa Nariaki of Mito. His brief was to observe

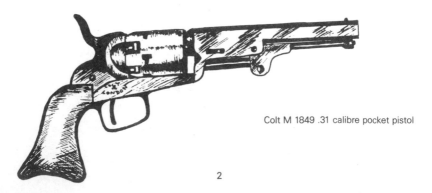

Colt M 1849 .31 calibre pocket pistol

Sai Hai commanders tasseled baton

the Kurofune black ships, especially the one encircled by a single red line. Its coming had been "leaked" by the Dutch at their free-port of Deshima.

It was now Tatsu No Toki, the Hour of the Dragon (7-9 a.m.) on the eight day of the seventh month (Fumidzuki) in the sixth year of Kayei (8th July 1853). Ikeda fingered the lilac silk ties on his russet iron Mempo face mask. Everyone from the humblest foot soldier to the Hatamoto standard bearers were literally armed to the teeth.

Lacquered armour and burnished brass gleamed as the sun rose higher in the sky. Beads of sweat formed and trickled into every crevice of the Samurai armour, soon the flies would attend to the dry salt. Even now, the humidity was choking.

On the Kurofune (black ship), the flagship ran up a message to her companions. This was answered by semaphore. At this, Ikeda motioned to his lieutenant, Noda Hisamori, a Samurai of about sixty years, sporting a fine white beard and wearing a white Hachimaki head band. Noda moved forward and drew his paper tasselled Saihai, he waved it once. From below came the boom of a great drum. The drummer was the only man not wearing full

Laquered iron mempo face mask

armour. He was naked save for a loincloth and a white sweat band. He held two long drumsticks, over three feet in length and four inches thick. He began to beat out a regular beat. The naked figure gleamed with sweat. The great signal drum, a circular pawlonia mon crest in its centre was all of eight feet in diameter. The hide resonated as the demon drummer beat out his secret code.

Ten miles from the coast, in a hollow in the side of a mountain, which acted as a huge ear, stood a lone Samurai. He was dressed in full armour, his great crested helmet rested on a nearby rock. In his hands he cradled a great conch shell with a gilded trumpet – like mouthpiece, the rest of the shell being held in a red silk net. The Samurai pricked his ears up, like a good dog scenting a rabbit. He brought the conch to his lips, waited for the last drum echo to fade, then blew a long wailing tone; once, twice, three times. As he blew, he moved the conch from left to right, willing the sound on to its destination.

In the Soto Zen temple at the foot of the mountain, the priests went peacefully about their contemplative life. The only jarring note in this serene picture was the terrifying figure of a Samurai warrior amidst the black-clad monks and priests. His lamellar armour was edged with purple and red silk. The brown lacquered breastplate being of the Yukinoshita Do form, which was said to withstand musket fire. As the long wailing tone of the conch bounced down the glades into the temple precincts, the Samurai, seated in the combat-ready posture of Tate Hiza, sprang up and walked positively towards a great wooden canopy. Within this structure was held the great bronze bell, used only on occasions of great religious significance.

4

The great bell, over fourteen feet high, hung from its canopy by a great hemp hawser. Cast into the body of the dark green bell, was the entire 600 verses of the Dai Hannya Sutra. Indeed it was said that when the six foot tree trunk hanging next to the bell, was swung to hit it, even the most evil soul was purified by the sound of all the Dai Hannya at once.

The Samurai grasped the great trunk with both his armoured hands and swung, once, twice. On the third swing, the great trunk contacted the bell with a vast explosion of sound. The Samurai grimaced as his ear-drums burst. He bit his lip until the blood came and trickled out of the black lacquered half Mempo mask. With determination and re-newed spirit he bravely fought through his pain and swung the tree trunk again and again, until blackness overtook him.

The sound of the Dai Hannya bell flowed down the cascades and torrents of a great river valley – a pure wall of sound bounced from side to side. Peasants fishing from the banks, paused and made obeisance to the Temple, for to them, the bell was the voice of God.

Halfway down the great river valley, beside a rocky precipice, was an ornately-carved wooden bridge. Its rails were painted with bright red lacquer, the posts topped with acorn-shaped bronze caps. From beneath a natural arch of trees strolled a Samurai bowman. He wore ornate purple and gold brocade breech Hakama, straw sandals bound on his feet. His left shoulder was bared, the simple brown Kimono tied safely with a length of sword binding. The long white bow curved as the radish-ended Karimata war arrow was nocked and drawn. The bowman bent back slightly; pointing the bow high to the sky. With a deep breath, the bow was drawn to its fullest tension. The Samurai bowman centred his spirit and as the time became right, he released the Karimata arrow. Shooting forth with a screaming whine like a thousand souls in torment, it winged its way upward; the sound of its passage floating on the wind.

On the outskirts of the great city of Edo, home of the Shogun and centre of his power-structure, crouched a group of four stern-faced boys. They could have been no older than thirteen years of age, but these were extraordinary times. Each of them was dressed in perfectly fitting battle armour and miniature Tachi-slung swords. As the Karimata whined its way to the heavens, they sprang to their tasks. A long bamboo tube, bound about with rough iron was stuck in the ground. Into this tube, two of the Samurai boys fed a six foot rocket. The third struck a flint and ignited some dry tinder which he handed to the fourth boy, who was clearly the leader of the group. The three stepped back and sat in lai Hiza. The leader then applied the burning tinder to the rocket's fuse. A brief pause was soon followed by a "whooshing" noise and the acrid smell of saltpetre gunpowder mix filled the air. The rocket sped upwards, it reached its zenith then fell back towards the earth. As it began to retard, the rocket exploded with a loud crack, like that of a maroon. Thus was the news of the black ship's arrival brought to Edo.

In a scene reminiscent of the news of Sekigahara's victory, two hundred and fifty years before, the entirety of Edo was spurred into action. Everything that could be blown or struck to make a noise, was utilised as the great city prepared for action. The temple bells rang, the roads and byeways were thronged with Samurai. Some drew their swords, and threw their scabbards into the dust – symbolic of the fact that they would not sheath them until victory was their's or until death took them. Toothless old men struggled into armour which had fitted them forty years before; picking up anything which could be used as a weapon, they prepared to sell their lives dearly. Samurai women gathered in ranks, the sleeves of their ornate Kimono tied back. In their frail hands; long naginata halberds, eager to taste foreign blood. Not since the days of the Kamikaze, had such a fervour gripped the land.

The sun began to set and the sky was suffused with an eerie glow, as a comet streaked the night sky – a portent. In the half glow, two words began to form on the lips of both Samurai and commoner until the very streets of Edo rang to their sound.

The taiko drum tolls out the
Black Ship's arrival

7

"Revere the Emperor, Expel the barbarian!" "Sonno! Joi! Sonno! Joi!"

Behind a stone pallisade, across a draw bridge, between a dry moat and a wall of spears and muskets, nestled the fire-proof Kura Godown of Tokugawa Nariaki, when in Edo, his priceless treasures were stored deep within this fire and earthquake-proof bunker. Stones, cut and shaped, bigger than the tallest Sumotori, fitted together with geometrical precision. Indeed, at the junctures, the fit was so tight that not even a single sheet of Hosho paper could pass through it. Pierced in this mighty edifice was a double span door, sheeted with rough iron and studded through with great bolts of tempered steel, each bearing Nariaki's personal cipher. Through the door and down stone flag steps, worn smooth by ten generations of Samurai feet. Along a corridor bounded by yet more of the geometrical stones. Across a hall which contained a robber's dream — fine suits of armour in lacquered boxes, priceless porcelain, swords and gold. Oh yes, more gold than two strong men could carry in forty days. Through this to a small dark chamber where the light of the sun never shone. The secret of secrets, accessible only to the most trusted of Samurai retainers. Twelve packing cases, bearing the seal of the Dutch Minheer at Deshima, contained the most secret items in the whole of Japan. To even breathe word of the existence was to invite death:

Items 1 to 6 — 100 Colt Model 1849 pocket revolvers and ammunition.

Items 7 to 10 — 1 prototype Gatling gun and parts.

Gold was indeed a past master.

Atop these boxes sat Tokugawa Nariaki's most trusted confidante, Sasano Mitsuyuki. He wore the breech hakama and hip armour. Save for a white Haramaki belly band, he was naked from the waist up. His subordinates sat around him in full armour, sweating quietly. A single taper lit the darkness. Sasano picked up one of the colts and with practised skill, spun the chamber. He cocked the hammer back and pointed the .31 calibre pistol at Eriguchi his aide. His finger tightened and the hammer fell. There was a slight flash as the percussion cap exploded — but no discharge. Sasano wished to make a point.

"With one finger you would be dead. Twenty years of Bugei training, all for nothing. Killed by a weapon it takes less time to learn than one takes to recite the 53 stations of the Tokkaido."

Eriguchi breathed a sigh of relief. Sasano continued.

"And what of this," he tapped the boxes which contained the prototype Gatling gun — "with this a cavalry charge is nothing. Castle doors are cut through, no sentry safe, even behind an emplacement. These are the weapons of the barbarian, they have

The war conch (Horagai)

no honour, but they are effective.

We stand like beggars at the gate of a new age. Barbarians seek our fair land from all sides, if not for our resources, then as a staging point for Tang." Here he referred to China, by the common character.

"We cannot sit idly by and let our ports become stock-piles of black stone to fire their ships.."

The great temple bell

Here, as ever, the intelligence networks, that had, at a price, managed to obtain restricted weapons, also obtained vital information about Perry's steam frigates.

"Tono?" said Eriguchi, who felt that the time was politic to suggest a solution.

"Tono, I most respectfully suggest that we seek the aid of the Metsuke."

"What?!" exploded Sasano; "no word of any of this must reach official channels. There are some Lords who would throw in their lot with the barbarians. And if it meant disgracing my Lord

Nariaki over these" – here he gestured to the packing cases – "they would do so. The scum. No, any action which we take to destroy this barbarian filth must be done the old way!"

"You mean with Nin?"

Here Eriguchi uttered a forbidden word. Two centuries of Bakufu Government had eradicated the last of the Ninja clans. Any records were confiscated and held at the great repository of written works in Kyoto. The families were scattered, or absorbed into the Metsuke – a kind of "all seeing eye" spy network, responsible for policing the minds of the people.

"What a scholar you are Eriguchi" said Sasano, angry that his glory had been stolen from him. "Yes, with Nin! For some time, our Lord Nariaki has feared this invasion. These are desperate times and they call for desperate measures. Not a hundred Ri (244 miles) from here in Koga, my Lord Nariaki has discovered the fifth generation successor to an ancient Ninja clan."

"Which one"? queried Eriguchi.

Sasano looked at him for a moment, silently marking him down for service in Hokkaido with the Ainu – too clever and loud for his own good. Sasano paused, then began again to speak.

"Those of you, who, like Eriguchi, have studied this secret facet of our past, will know of whom I speak. But for those of you who are not so familiar, I will outline the situation. When the Divine Toshogu Tokugawa Ieyasu claimed victory at Sekigahara and Osaka, Japan, as you know, became the unified state which you see today. The great masters of deception and death – the Ninja clans – were almost as powerful as Lord Tokugawa Ieyasu. Of course, this state of things could not continue. One by one, by both deceit and direct action, the once proud Ninja clans were

destroyed and destroyed bloodily. By all accounts, they were terrible times. Only one man, a most unusual man, by the name of Tada, managed to survive this and became, as some say, "the Shogun's Ninja". Eventually he lead the Metsuke in the great reforms that make the state which we see today. But like all great men, he was flawed; his weakness was his desire for revenge. One day he ordered a party of his loyal retainers; took ship and sailed off to Satsuma, from whence they never returned. But Tada was a careful man; he left a son — secret and safe, out of public view. Thus was the line continued up to today. It is Tada Hisamori who continues the tradition of the Tomokatsu Ryu Ninja."

"So" said Eriguchi, finally sealing his fate, "Our Lord Nariaki plans to use the Ninja skills to dispatch the barbarians."

"Quite so" snapped Sasano, again raising the Colt pistol. He pointed it at Eriguchi's armoured chest. The hammer clicked back, then, as Eriguchi was in mid-sentence, the trigger pulled, the hammer fell and one and a half ounces of lead smashed through the breast-plate. As the bullet tore through the heart muscles, Eriguchi's body was picked up like a wooden Kokeshi doll. His lifeless body bounced against the geometrically carved stones and finally came to rest between wall and packing cases.

"Traitor!" spat Sasano.

Not one of the Samurai made or even thought of daring to make, any comment about the situation. Sasano stood upon the packing case.

"Now we have the path set for us. The time is right. We have nothing to lose but all to gain. Koga awaits us. Let us go!"

the black brotherhood

"Nukitsuke! Kiritsuke! Chiburi! Noto!"

"Draw, Cut, Clean, Sheath!" The command was repeated and repeated, echoing from the white walls of the Castle Keep. One hundred black-clad ninja went through the intricate sword exercises that characterised the ninja's Iai Jutsu and Ken Jutsu. To a Samurai, trained in the classical forms of swordsmanship, the ninja appeared most unorthodox — but this was an intended impression. A ninja drew his straight single-edged sword overhand from the matt black scabbard strapped to his back across the right shoulder and left hip. An unorthodox method which had sealed the fate of many an unwary Samurai sentry. A classical warrior would expect a sword to be drawn crosswise, forward from the left hip. When a sword materialises from the right shoulder, the only words on the lips of an unwitting victim might be — "But that's not right!". Whatever the case, they would be his last words. The grip was also a most curious affair, instead of gripping with the thumb close to the guard as was the normal right hand position, this was reversed so that the smallest finger was close to the guard. The left hand held the sword in the normal manner, at the end of the hilt, the small finger gripping the pommel, or in certain cases, the length of rope and small weight similar to the style of Kusarigama, or the Kyoketsu Shoge.

Closer observation of the hundred ninja warriors, showed that some were indeed wielding swords with rope weights. What was also apparent from their training, was the presence, strapped around each wrist, of a black cotton strap, containing a number of lead musket balls, weighing about 4 kilograms each strap. A similar device around the waist weighed a massive 10 kilograms, two more around the ankles weighed 6 kilograms each. These

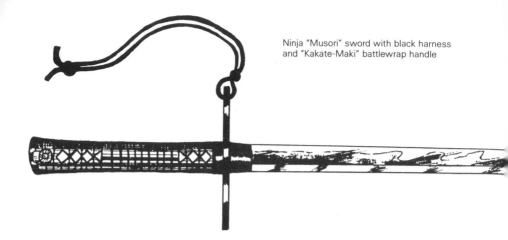

Ninja "Musori" sword with black harness and "Kakate-Maki" battlewrap handle

were worn at all times for training, except for swimming. The reason was austere but effective, once removed the speed and power generated was truly formidable.

"Yame!" boomed out the commander. He was attired in the same clothing as the other men, only his power of spirit marked him apart from his followers. Silently, a hundred blades were sheathed. The ninja formed a great circle around the leader. At a pre-arranged signal, twenty of the ninja detached themselves from the group. They quickly returned, laden with six foot lengths of green bamboo.

A circle of twenty bamboo posts, all at least 4 inches thick, were placed in holes around the leader. At a right angle, a line of forty poles were spaced about three feet apart, at the end of this line, four, eighteen inch thick bundles of straw were stood on special wooden stands, which propped these bundles up to chest height. The damp straw smelled sweetly of the fields and of a good harvest the year before.

At another pre-arranged command, the circle of a hundred ninja fanned back to the perimeter of the courtyard. Almost, as if at a silent signal, all sat down in Tate Hiza. For the first time, they were allowed to remove their black head coverings revealing brigandine chain head-bands. These head-bands were not removed, but the hundred ninja, fifty of whom were women, the Kunoichi, wiped the sweat of ten hours unbroken training from their eyes.

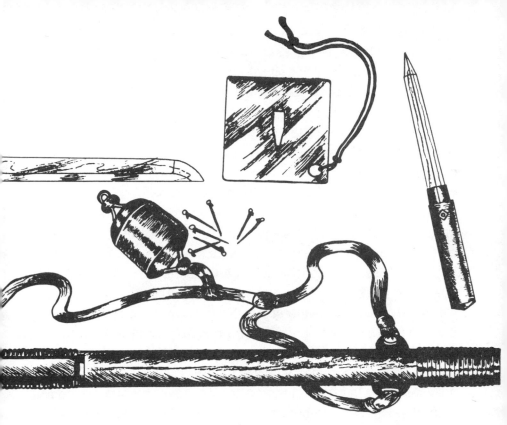

Then all were silent — watching and waiting. The leader squatted in the centre of his green bamboo compound. He slowly brought his black gloved hands together and made the symbolic Mudra incantation known as Kankuji. He formed his fingers into an intricate pattern and then clapped his hands twice. With the pen of his imagination, he exorcised all minus elements from his mind and carefully drew the Kanji character for victory on the palms of his hands. To seal this, he clapped twice more and intoned the secret Vajraken Sutra of Tomokatsu Ryu Ninja. There was then eerie silence. The birds in the eaves of the great castle in the West were strangely silent, as if some giant hand had cupped them and drawn them away — the almost tangible silence pervaded everything. All eyes were on the black-clad figure in the centre of the circle.

From the half-crouch of Iai Hiza, the commander leaped forward, his legs propelling him smoothly, high into the air. As he rose, his right hand snaked over his shoulder to reach the hilt of his ninja sword. As his feet, encased in split-toed boots, landed softly, the sword was out and had simultaneously cut the first bamboo, a smooth diagonal cut which started to ooze sap water even as the sword continued in its arc. The commander's body twisted and the ninja sword bit into the second bamboo. On the up-cut, the bamboo toppled. As the heavy length of bamboo began to fall, the commander deftly sidestepped, cutting horizontally. His action was so fast and so sure, that before the first bamboo had hit the floor, the fifth was being cut. The bamboo was cut cleanly, releasing the air inside the tube with a sound, Tok! The commander crouched low, then sprang high. As he made his way around the circle, the Musori straight blade cut and slashed in a blur of action. The commander cut the twentieth, as the bamboo toppled he swiftly reversed the blade and cut the falling tube in two. For a brief second the commander lined up in front of the row of forty. With a massive side-step he leaped obliquely forward, the first two bundles fell, cut cleanly with a horizontal cut. With a roll, he noiselessly hit the ground in front of the next bamboo, his body twined around the bamboo and sword mercilessly cleft the green tube. To the onlookers, it was apparent that against a sentry, this turning cut from below would be absolutely effective. Ninja science had evolved the theory that in a dark or half-light situation, a lone sentry pays most attention to the areas behind his right ear. Indeed it is a curious phenomena displayed many times, in many different places, that a lone sentry is most cautious, almost expecting attack from behind to the right. This does vary, with some sentries alert to and expecting attack from the left, but it is a rare sentry who expects an attack from underneath.

With quiet ferocity, the commander leaped and dived; jumped and fell until the fortieth bamboo in the line stood alone. Forsaking his keen blade, the commander's open right hand thrust forward. He gripped the thick green stem of the bamboo — earthing his spirit — the forces of great power channels within the ninja's body co-ordinated. The bamboo cracked, giving up the air contained in it with a high-pitched whine. The commander's hand snaked back to his sword, the crushed bamboo stem wavered for

1. Tobi Tameshigiri   2. Gyaku Tameshigiri   3. Ryote Tameshigiri

a moment then began to topple; half-way in its downward movement, the commander's sword sliced it cleanly. A gasp of ad-
miration came from one of the ninja, who briefly forgot his iron self
control. The commander paid this no heed, instead he stepped
forward to the straw bales. Quickly adopting the straddle leg
stance which some call Jigotai, he readied his sword in a high
position, similar to Hassō Nō Kamae. Without any further preparation, he sliced across in the cut known as Kesa Giri – after the Zen
priest's bib, a garment which rests upon one shoulder and the
opposite hip. The straw parted cleanly as his blade bit through in a
centrifugal arc. At the deep point of the cut, the commander
dropped his hips slightly – the effect was to propel the blade
cleanly out of the opposite side of the bale. The commander deftly
stepped over the cut straw and stood with the next two bales on
either side of him. He held the Musori blade out in front of him,
edge downwards, he then turned the blade through 90° so the
cutting edge was on the horizontal. Then for the first time, he
released the awesome Ninja Kiai – it was legend that this could
stun the very birds from the trees. As the Kiai welled from his
lower stomach in a deep growl, the blade moved blindingly fast;
first left then right, returning to an unwavering dead stop at
exactly the instant that the Kiai ended. The two bales split like
over-ripe fruit, showering a fine mist of grass seeds into the air.
Slowly and deliberately, the commander walked to the fourth and
final bale. He stood in front of it, again in Jigotai, the sword in
Hassō Nō Kamae, ready to cut Kesa. This time he brushed the
blade carressingly across the straw. A movement so quick that

some must surely have missed it. The sword returned to Hassō Nō Kamae. He sheathed the sword into the black harness, then slowly looked around, his eyes black as the barrels of a hand cannon under the "eaves" of his black combat hood.

There was an uncomfortable silence. A few ninja wondered why he had not sliced the fourth and last straw bale. The weaker may have even begun to doubt the commanders's skill, for surely he had failed the final test. But, as in life, the obvious is rarely the truth. The commander removed his black hood with a flourish, a great booming laugh echoed as he flicked the hood at the straw bale. The bale fell cleanly apart, cascades of cut straw showering around the three-legged hardwood stand. So swift and powerful had his final cut been that the human eye had not registered it. Indeed it was said that one might be cut by it and still live, until the body is moved – whatever the truth of this, it certainly was a devastating movement.

For the first time, the commander spoke, his voice was slow and measured, hardly betraying the exertion of the movements he had just completed.

"My loyal retainers; sons and daughters of the truth that is Tomokatsu Ryu I congratulate you. Today our training is at an end, many have died in the course of this endeavour and I offer a prayer to their souls. Our lives are but a brief shadow; so I say, let us be proud and stand in the sun. Our's is the legacy of four centuries; unbroken it shall continue. Our's is the legacy of Grand Master Tada – may his soul find rest wherever it can."

The commander brought his gloved hands together in the Mudra sign for spiritual cleansing. The hundred strong survivors; graduates if you will; out of the two hundred and fifty who had commenced the secret course eight months previously, also made the Mudra sign for spiritual cleansing as they stood in a circle, and for a brief second, remembered friends and lovers, some of whom had died by their hands in the training. Ninja training was training for death as well as life, it did not countenance failure, death was the only way out of its brotherhood.

Outside the walled enclosure, a Taiko drum beat five times.

A Ninja demonstrates the unorthodox grip with his "Musori" blade

The great camphor wood gates moved slowly on their massive hinges. The sound of horses' hooves on the great winding stone steps, as the envoy and his entourage clattered into the secret place. At the rear, suspended from great laquered poles, swung the laquered carrying chest, emblazened with the personal seal of the Tokugawa Nariaki. The burly polemen were clad in Tatami Gosuku folding armour and bore Chiisa Katana thrust through their sashes.

Sasano, the envoy, reigned in the pure white stallion bred in Soma. It was bedecked with vermillion and gold battle armour and a great plate, fashioned like a rain dragon was fixed to its head. The envoy nudged the gilded iron "abumi" stirrup which encased his right foot like a boot; into the horse's flank. The animal shied slightly, then moved over, side-trotting as it had been schooled to do, until it was less than an arm's length from the commander.

"Tada Hisamori, well done, you seem to have trained them well."

Tada felt contempt for this man; his answer was crisp.

"I only brought out that which was already within."

"Well said! It is said that a true Ninja fears nothing, not even death itself."

"There are many fears" replied Tada, "Some you know and some you may not know until they grasp you. A Ninja fears much, but fear does not stop him."

"Even in the face of death?"

Tada knew exactly what the envoy was trying to do and he vainly tried to re-direct the conversation.

"Even in death?" persisted the envoy.

Recognising the impasse which was developing, Tada relented.

"Yes, even in death."

The envoy, Sasano smiled a most evil smile. He pointed to one of the Kunoichi.

"You, step forward."

The tiny Kunoichi stepped forward from her position in the circle of ninja.

The "Makiwara" true test of sword skill

The single bamboo tube test of the true cut!

21

"Well, my dear, I'm told that a true ninja will not be stopped even in the face of death. Is that so?"

The Kunoichi glanced at Tada, her commander. His face was stern. He bowed slightly, the girl turned to look the envoy squarely in the eye.

"That is so" she said.

This response visibly disturbed the envoy. From a recess in his saddle, he drew the colt pistol, which he pointed straight at her. The Kunoichi Ninja did not move.

The force of the pistol shot which caught her squarely in the gap between her eyebrows, spun her over and down, she was dead before the ground cradled her. Not one of the ninja outwardly registered any emotion. Tada's face remained impassive.

"Well that was truly impressive" said Sasano, as he holstered his "toy".

Tada walked forward and placed his hand on the laquered iron ankle armour. His knuckles went white as he squeezed. The iron began to buckle, biting into the envoy's flesh. Sasano was too petrified even to scream. To outsiders it appeared that he and Tada were deep in conference, for the commander's face and tone belied his words, as softly he cooed,

"Your demonstration is very impressive envoy Sasano, but no-one debases my ninja. These words are between you and I. When we have accomplished the great task, I intend to find you. I intend to cut off your arms and legs, I will not kill you outright, but you will die a thousand deaths before the final release."

With these words, Tada smiled in a most disconcerting way.

The envoy gave Tada the scroll containing his orders and turned his horse around, spurring it off through the gates. As he

Hand cannon

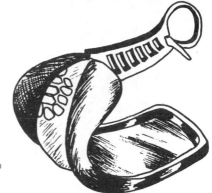

Iron abumi stirrup

went, he scattered the laquer boxes, one of which spilled open, revealing boxes containing the colt pocket pistols. For those who could read Barbarian script, the writing on the side of the boxes gave the country of manufacture — London. Many colt pistols, originated, under licence, from the London gun houses.

With great reverence, the ninja picked up the body of the fallen Kunoichi. Carrying her shoulder high on a makeshift platform of swords, they slowly bore her away from the field. It is a curious thing, and one not easily explained; that in moments of great stress, the ninja fuse together and act as one — silently. So close is their understanding that it defies mere words.

Left alone, Tada Hisamori, heir to the Tomokatsu Ryu Ninja, carefully unrolled the Emaki scroll outlining the precise plan for the new ninja to do their best. Sonno Joi — revere the Emperor, Expel the Barbarian.

The sun fell behind the high keep and the courtyard was suddenly dark. Tada rolled up the scroll and intoned the fragments of the words of the way:—

"The darkness surrounds me
I am clothed in night."

Breaking from his reverie he called for Songoro, the dwarf — as tall as the pommel of a Katana, but with the heart and mind of a bear. He could skilfully wield a jo of iron that a Sumotori would have difficulty in lifting. In a trice, the tiny figure of Songoro was with him. Tada knelt down and began to explain the beginning of the end —

An hour later, with the knowledge which hot coals would not drag out of him, Songoro set off on his mission.

shades of black

"Down the streets of shame, a dark horseman rode, his spearpoint red with traitor's blood" – the sound of a Shoji screen being hastily drawn, caused Inada Koichi, personal equerry to Ii Naosuke, the Shogun's strongman, to look up from the lurid novel which he was reading. It was typical of the woodblock printed books extolling Samurai virtue and, more popularly, Samurai pornography. Quickly closing the book, Inada slipped it inside his Kimono. He busied himself instead with an official report to Lord Ii. The clatter grew louder and louder as screens hastily slid open, only to close shortly after with a hollow "clack".

Feet enclosed in split-toed tabi socks, scampered up the polished wood floors of the vast country house some 30 Ri (78 miles) west of Edo, that was the nerve centre of Lord Ii Naosuke's power structure. He played the political game – the stakes were high, but the rewards were immeasurably higher. Like his forbears who had thrown in their lot with Ieyasu at Sekigahara, whose Red Devils were the scourge of the Shōgun's enemies; so too was Ii Naosuke. He fully realised that the isolation of two and a half centuries must end, rather than crying 'havoc' and loosing the dogs of war as Tokugawa Nariaki wanted, the coming of the black ships was long-awaited by Lord Ii. For him and his adherents, the new order would be one of great profit. The Shōgun would be the fountain head of the new age, and the Emperor would be pushed even further into the background.

With a swish and a clatter, the final Shoji screen was passed. There came a discreet knock and with great solemnity, the fusuma door, bearing the moon and fox motif was silently drawn open.

"Tono" said a Samurai of middle rank, "We are in receipt of

Manrikigusari Kama

news from Edo."

Inada, the equerry, put down the official document which he was pretending to read —

"Bid him enter."

The Samurai bowed low and went off to fetch the messenger. Inada quickly pulled a small circular mirror out and licking his index finger, he smoothed his eyebrows, patted stray hairs back into his raven black Chomage top knot and straightened the folds of his Kimono. He thrust the black laquer scabbard of the Wakizashi short sword into his belt. With his left hand holding the guard of the sword, his right hand held a small Uchiwa fan — apeing the style of his Lord, Master Ii. On his Lord it was magnificent, on Inada, it was pathetic!

A few minutes passed, then with a familiar rattle, the smooth wooden shoji opened and closed along the length of the building. The fusuma drew open to reveal a messenger. He was dressed in immaculate grey kimono and hakama, bearing the Ii crest.

The Omi Yari

Knowing the vanity of Inada of old; the messenger had taken the precaution of changing into the clean clothes provided for him by the middle-rank Samurai. A normal commander would be eager to hear a messenger's news — but not Inada — he insisted upon protocol at all times.

The messenger bowed low. Inada curtly returned the bow, and standing up, he walked to the Shoji screen which separated the garden from the room. With a flourish, he pulled the screen open. The room grew brighter as the mid-day light flooded in.

"Attend me" he said, walking out on to the polished wooden verandah.

He bent forward to slip on the pair of wooden geta clogs which rested on a huge stone step about 9 inches lower than the verandah. He then strolled into the garden, leaving the messenger to hastily don another pair of geta and follow behind.

Down a stone and fine pebble path they walked, to a small water butt, in the shape of a Zeni coin. The water was held in the

square recess at its centre, atop it was bamboo water dipper, resting upon three lengths of bamboo tube. Inada dipped into the water butt and drew out a dipper-full. He carefully poured the water over the false beach of grey/green pebbles brought all the way from Sado Island. With the affected stare of the uncultured aiming for what they fondly believe culture to be; he watched the spray of water from the dipper turn the dry stones into many faceted jewels.

The messenger walked up behind Inada. He had heard that Inada was a martinet, but he had not expected such a petty, vain, affected man. His sense of self-preservation, stayed his tongue, he remained silent, awaiting Inada.

"Charming, don't you think?" said Inada, pointing to the wet stones.

"Indeed" replied the messenger diplomatically.

"Yes" said Inada, "I often liken their glistening smoothness to the eye of the 31st Bodhisatva at Sanju Sangendo."

This rubbish continued for a full ten minutes. Then with self-conceited grandeur, Inada leant against a low stone wall, turning his face to the sun —

"Tell me, my dear. You have some news for me?"

The messenger bit his tongue hard. With the salt-iron taste of his own blood, and feeling shame that a Samurai could be brought so low.

Iron tekko ninja knuckleduster

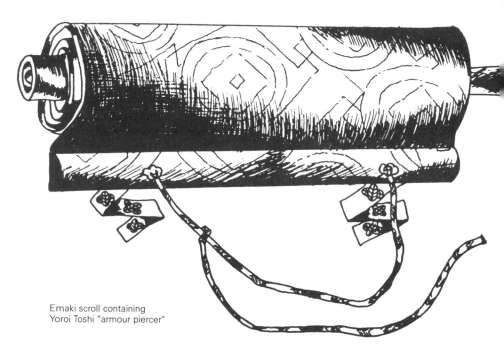

Emaki scroll containing
Yoroi Toshi "armour piercer"

"Yes, Tono. The Kurofune black ships are at anchor at Uraga. They are to send a party ashore in two days time. The Daimyo at Kurihama is to accept any messages they are ordered to bring. It is rumoured that the Sonno Joi supporters will be up to something."

Inada moved his face out of the direct glare of the sun.

"So Tokugawa Nariaki's up to his old tricks again. You have done well to be so swift."

The messenger said nothing.

Inada continued —

"Take a fresh horse and ride to the Sugiyama Temple. Give the gateman this."

From our of the fold of his Kimono, he brought the octagonal bronze medallion into which he pressed a curious design. As he did so, the lurid woodblock-printed book fell out and opened at his feet, displaying its contents for the messenger to see; being shrewd, he did not notice. Instead, he gazed into the middle distance.

"By your command!" said the messenger.

He placed the octagonal medallion in his carrying pouch, worn

under his hakama, much in the style of the old Portuguese. He turned and left.

Inada watched him walk away, admiring his broad shoulders. Glancing down, he noticed the book and scrabbled to pick it up before any of his servants appeared to notice. He need not have worried, his private garden was empty; save for the watchful eyes of Songoro, who was hiding in a large pot used for specimen bamboo. He was dressed in a green and yellow-striped ninja combat suit, the reverse side of the black night combat suit. Covered with bamboo leaves, he was undetectable. He watched and waited.

Soon Inada walked back to the Zelkova wood verandah, took off his wooden geta and strolled back into the interior. The Shoji screens closed, once again the garden was silent. Songoro did not stir, ninja intelligence transcended the physical. Soon the unspoken warning made itself clear – a Yojimbo bodyguard checked the garden on his 'rounds'. Even when these checks seemed sporadic, there was a psychology and a timing to them. Songoro waited again, then "testing the air" as the ninja called it, he felt with his senses, for any unnatural feeling – "Kimochi". There was no such feeling, all seemed harmonious. Slowly Songoro relocated his hips and shoulder joints. As he emerged from the seemingly tiny hide-out, he took a deep breath; first fully expelling

Bo and Hanbo

Uchiwa fan with spike shuriken

the stale air from his lungs, for he had slowed his breathing cycle and heartbeat. In the distance, Songoro heard the clatter of the messenger's horse as he sped to the Sugiyama Temple bearing the octagonal medallion with the secret code.

Songoro's job was almost done. All that remained was for him to retrieve the bamboo tube which he had deftly hidden high up in a maple tree. Like the monkey King of legend, Songoro clambered up through the dark branches of the old tree. He retrieved the tube from the topmost boughs. Carefully he removed the tiny messenger bird. After attaching the coded message to the bird's leg, he let it soar heavenwards. He watched as the bird soared and dipped to take its bearings before flying off to master Tada at the castle stronghold. Whilst still in the shadows of the tree, Songoro reversed his combat suit and awaited the night.

As the stone Ishidoro lanterns in the garden were lit, throwing out a soft aura of light, the night bugs and fire flies swayed to and fro. Now was the time for Songoro to leave. The dull glint of his iron jo would be as unnoticed as a distant firefly by all but the most skilful of guards. Gently, slowly, the tiny ninja slithered shadow-like down the trunk of the tree. He moved across the garden,

The Kaga Mitsu Je in action

Sangoro the dwarf ninja disables a Samurai guard using an iron Jo

keeping to the shadows at all times. He traversed the bamboo fence by way of the Sode Gaki side fence. He found himself in a small enclosure; blending with the stone of one wall, he inched his way across. Bright light flooded the small square, as a Shoji flew open. With one bound, a scribe of the second order leaped out, brandishing an emaki scroll as if it were a sword. The scribe waved it in the air in a silent battle against imaginary opponents. Songoro watched incredulously as the silent battle unfolded. There was a click and the scribe drew a beautifully forged Yoroi toshi armour-piercer from a secret partition in the handle of the scroll. He brandished it, flashing it left and right; then lunging forward, impaled it in a wooden pillar. Songoro peered through the gloom and saw that the pillar was tattered from many such attacks. Evidently the scribe who aspired to be a Samurai warrior, practised regularly. Leaving the armour-piercer quivering in the post, the scribe then withdrew an uchiwa fan. From its handle he pulled a ring spike shuriken. Turning once, he sent this spinning through the air to land in the undergrowth. The scribe swore quietly, he would have to wait until daylight to retrieve the shuriken. He now reached into the room and brought out one of his fude brushes. With a deft twist, the brush was removed to reveal a hollow tube containing ten hari needle-like shuriken. These he

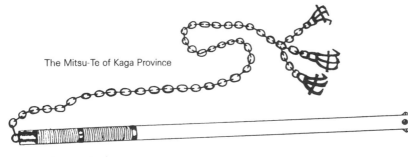

The Mitsu-Te of Kaga Province

dispatched in quick succession at the pillar, most of them stuck in their target. Reasonably well pleased with himself, he collected the weapons together and stepped back into the room. The Shoji dashed shut as the make-believe Samurai returned to the business of writing out and conveyancing reports.

Songoro had watched the whole spectacle in a state of bemusement at the vagaries of human nature. He padded forward, under the verandah and down the dusty underside of the house. Chinks of light gleamed through in places where boards did not fit on the square. As he crawled through; so silently that even the mice who rule this subterranean kingdom were undisturbed, Songoro heard the sounds that mapped out his progress – the swish of the scribe's brush on paper, the sharp rap as a Shoji chess piece was placed on its wooden board, the mewing sound as a courtesan entertained her "husband" for the hour. Then a more sinister sound, as a Samurai honed his sword blade skilfully on a wet stone in the armoury. All these, Songoro passed under before emerging on the other side of the building.

The scribe's fude-brush holds a few surprises

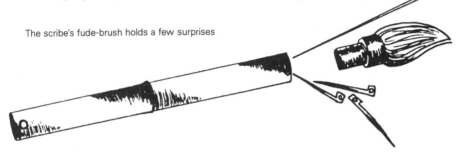

Silently he crossed to the stable block, passing down the back of the buildings, past a quietly steaming pile of manure. Across the vegetable garden, in and out of the neat lines of well-tended produce. In the velvet blackness, Songoro came upon a paved area, a path that led to the carp pond. He sensed that something was not right. With a side-step he moved to hug the side of a tree as a Samurai with a fish skewered on a slither of bamboo, walked past. The Samurai must have been better than the normal stock, for he sensed Songoro's presence and started to turn. As he did so, Songoro's iron jo caught him in the soft part underneath the breast bone. Leaping up and around, Songoro executed the swallow tail reverse, which involved a circling jump and strike. It was developed in Kaga Province for use with the Mitsu-te chain staff. At the peak of the movement, Songoro's jo shot out and caught the already slumping Samurai hard under the left ear, but

not hard enough to break skin or bone. Just hard enough for Songoro to escape, leaving the Samurai to "come to" with the biggest headache since the brewmaster's son's wedding.

Songoro looked down at the Samurai, who by reflex, had drawn his sword. He carefully replaced the sword in its scabbard, picked up the skewered fish and placed it in the Samurai's right hand; put a large pebble on his chest and a bough across his neck. The fancies of a night would be put down to no more than a mishap with a falling branch — remembering his drawn sword, would result in a hand holding a fish. Songoro's escape would be safeguarded.

Shaking the dust of the Ii stronghold from his feet, Songoro struck out across country to return by a circuitous route, in case of pursuit. As Songoro steadily plodded up the foothills, his iron jo stood him in good stead as a mountain staff. He remembered tramping up the slopes of Sakurajima, far away in Kyushu, as a boy. His father had thought that it would encourage the dwarf to grow. It did not make him increase in height but it had broadened his back and strengthened his spirit. Far away from Songoro's mountain reverie, the messenger spurred his horse onwards to the Sugiyama Temple.

the raven wing, black as night

Long before its human messenger had reached the precincts of Sugiyama Temple, the messenger bird had winged its way to Tada Hisamori, Master of the new ninja. After hastily translating Songoro's coded message, he despatched a surveillance team to observe and report on the events at Sugiyama Temple.

Unfortunately events were proceeding faster than Tada had anticipated. The news soon came that Perry the Barbarian had actually set foot upon Japanese soil and had marched at the head of a marine band, to the appointed place where the headman at Kurihama had accepted letters from the Barbarbian President Philmore (Firumo, as the scribes called him) to the Emperor. By political necessity, they would never reach the Emperor.

The time was right, Tada Hisamori despatched a further twenty ninja to travel north on an assassination mission, which, if successful, would result in a major defeat for the li supporters. Let us draw a veil across this action now and return to the hills near Sugiyama......

Nestling amongst their deep green abundance, lay the temple of Sugiyama, built five hundred years previously and dedicated to the Amida Buddha. It had remained a peaceful mountain haven,

The iron strength jars

The iron swords

the sound of bells echoed through the multi-hued green. Wood smoke mixed with fine mist and the plaintiff sound of a Shaku Hachi flute completed the scene of idyllic tranquillity.

The messenger rode up a road made of rock scalpings; his Kimono bathed in sweat. He finally reined in his horse before the great cypress wood gate posts, bound with the great bronze cappings cast four centuries before. He dismounted. He had obviously been expected, for a young monk came out, his black robes contrasting sharply with the sheen of his bald head. In his hand he bore a white wood pitcher, atop which, rested a slender bamboo dipper. Close behind him came a lay brother who took charge of the foaming horse. The messenger gratefully accepted the offer of water, drinking, but not too deeply, the cool, crystal liquid.

Now refreshed, he asked the young monk where the gate-man was. The young monk, deliberately forbidden to speak, as a spiritual exercise, delicately pointed to where the gatekeeper stood waiting. The messenger walked towards him, his straw sandals releasing the piquant fragrance of crushed moss as he walked over it. The gatekeeper was as broad as he was tall. He was dressed as a monk but his face had a certain expression, which the messenger could not exactly place.

A huge hand was extended, into which the messenger placed the medallion. The hand closed and the medallion was completely enclosed within it. The gateman turned, the gate slammed shut, leaving the messenger outside. He looked up at the great gates and heard a regular beating sound, not being able to identify the sound; he turned away. He was confronted by the lay brother who led a fresh horse. The messenger mounted it and was then

The fists and feet clenched into iron

handed an ornately folded piece of Hosho paper. This he un-wrapped. In delicate red ink was the character for Edo. Having nothing better to do, he turned and spurred his horse back down the stone road in the direction of the capital of Edo.

No sooner had the clatter of horse's hooves died away than high up in the wooded hills surrounding the temple; dark shadows swayed to and fro as the gentle breezes wafted the topmost branches. Hanging precariously from these swaying boughs were Tada's intelligence-gathering team. They were ninja, but their main skills did not lay exclusively with weaponry — more with the cataloguing and collating of observed phenomena. Try as they might, to go for the high ground, at no point was there anything that gave access into the inner courtyard. One item that did not seem in keeping with the outwardly pious appearance was a high watch tower, standing on three tall tree trunks, there was a single pole with a long white streamer on top of it. Below that was a single bell of about two feet diameter. Even more curious was a man dressed in monk's robes seated within striking distance of the bell. Strangest of all was that this man had a full head of hair,

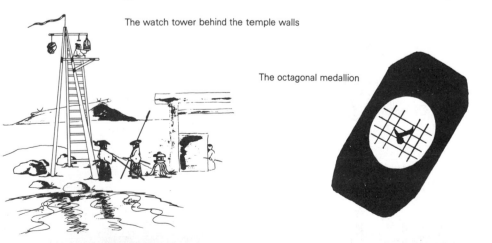
The watch tower behind the temple walls

The octagonal medallion

The striking post and hanging bag

dressed in the Samurai fashion. Communicating by imitating animal sounds, the ninjas decided that they must get closer; but they would wait until dark.

Had they been able to follow the gatekeeper into the compound, a most mysterious sight would have been unfolded to them. Beyond the cloister buildings, where the majority of monks were housed; was a number of low buildings, flanked by a square of earth, beaten rock hard by years of hardened feet. In this courtyard, the reason for the young monk's silence and the gatekeeper's reticence could be seen. Thirty men, naked from the waist up; wearing breech hakama and with their hair dressed in Samurai fashion, trained in a most unorthodox manner. They were divided into five groups of six, some performing and some correcting. There did not seem to be any overall leader. The reason for the silence became apparent when they spoke – although in

The test

Japanese, they spoke with a strong Okinawan accent. They hailed from Naha and Shuri and had been recruited as mercenaries by a middle-ranking Samurai of the Shimazu Han, under the strictest security and had been shipped to the Japanese mainland. They were the third generation of the line of Gushi and Sakiyama who had studied Kempo from Ku Shan Ku, the Chinese. They were glad to be paid so highly for the opportunity to kill a few Japanese or a few barbarians, the difference mattered little. At the end they had been promised land and money back on Okinawa, for them or for their families.

Their training was both brutal and severe. No punches or kicks were pulled and throws were made with full hip rotation. A normal man would be killed on the instant that the calloused fist or foot made contact, but not these men. Their bodies were rock hard and their spirits like steel. They worked together as a single unit, the weakness of one member was the weakness of the whole group, therefore, the strengths of all were kept at a peak. The separate groups practiced what must have seemed very strange to a Japanese. Great cast iron jars filled with water or sand were picked up with the thumb and fingers and lifted to shoulder height. Using special breathing patterns, coupled with tensing and relaxing the body as the performer stepped forward in the S patterned hour glass stance that they favour for such practice. Yet another group were working on tree trunks set deep in the ground, around which were wrapped several thicknesses of rice straw rope. Hanging next to the posts was a large bag made of thick cotton, it was full of heavily packed corn husks. The action was quite simple, but devastating. First, the tree trunk received a tremendous punch or strike — full-force, from either knuckles or straight

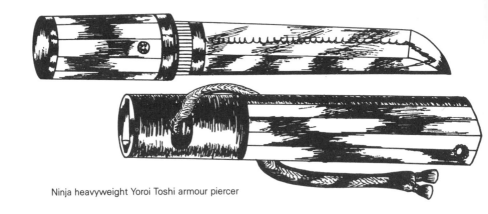

Ninja heavyweight Yoroi Toshi armour piercer

fingers. The bag was then kicked hard with either the bunched toes or a knee. So forceful and penetrating were these, that the bag was often pierced, cascading the striker with a spray of fine white dust and corn husks. This usually brought a burst of good-natured applause from the other members of their group.

The third unit were practicing in a circle. A piece of iron, cast in the shape of a carp's mouth and weighing over three hundred pounds, was tossed around the circle. It was sometimes caught squarely on the shoulders, twisted first one side, then the other, then picked up with a grasping action in either one or two hands. It was then flicked to the next in line. Thus in random pattern or in order, the circle was completed and a speed was built up, faster and faster. At odd times, one of the group would lose rhythm and the iron Koiguchi Carpmouth would hit bone with a sickening crunch. Such mistakes were shrugged off and oft times, blood poured down arms and faces unhindered.

The fourth group were practicing a most unlikely exercise for such powerfully-built men. A taut rope, stretched at an angle up to a fixing about twenty feet up in the air, much in the manner of a ship's line hawser. Up this incline, the Okinawans skilfully walked, their calloused feet acting like a second pair of gripping hands, as they deftly clambered up and down. Alternatively, they practiced carrying heavy weights up and down. As another exercise, they walked to the top of the rope, to leap off, landing like a cat from a height that would shatter the legs of a normal man.

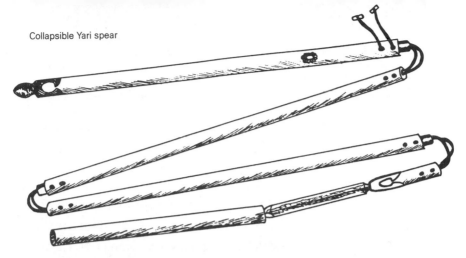

Collapsible Yari spear

The fifth group practiced by far the strangest exercise of all. With machine-like precision, they fought an imaginary battle with many adversaries, as they drilled through the complexities of Kata. Often one person would perform the Kata whilst his peers would observe the performer. At various points in the execution of the form, he would be stopped and whilst maintaining his last posture, would be punched and kicked by the other members of the group. He would be attacked from all sides and at every part of his body – even the groin area was allowed. All these were absorbed as though no more than a mild pat. With one almighty cross jaw reverse punch, the performer's head was rocked violently – spraying a shower of sweat in all directions. By weathering such onslaughts, the ultimate truth of their training was expressed.

Into this scene the gatekeeper strode. He still clutched the octagonal medallion with the curious cypher. By his bearing and the behaviour of the thirty Okinawans, this man was clearly the leader. In the rural Okinawan accent, he called the whole group together.

"Brothers, we have the sign, when the raven's wing darkens the sky (nightfall) together with our aquaintances –"

He gestured with his thumb to the outer compound, where a battalion of spear men, all mercenaries were quartered. All were highly skilled, perfecting their skills by stealth on the mainland of China, where life was cheap. A war-lord could hire a party of fanatics to fight his war. They had scant regard with victory or defeat, just wishing to fight and kill. Their apprenticeship was as complete as that of the Okinawans and they thirsted for the fight.

"Still time for some extra training" said the Okinawans' leader.

He picked up two gigantic cast iron weights, fashioned like Suburito swords. With one in each he brandished and swung his arms as he performed the intricacies of the deep-breathing Kata. Gnarled toes crushed the hard-packed earth, spraying up a fine dust. From the depths of his spirit came a mighty rumbling sound. It swelled in intensity. One by one, his followers took up the shout resulting in a cacophony of sound which seemed to shake the very foundations of the temple.

To the ninja, moving stealthily for better viewing positions, the tumultuous shout from within the temple confirmed their suspicions. Although as yet unseen, the threat was tangible. An observant guard in the temple compound might have noticed four tiny birds flying up and away in a loose formation. The ninja would wait and watch, they now knew that their mission was not in vain.

Treading the hawser

the furnace of shame

With a fiery blast, culminating in a white spume of hot steam, the great engine of the "Mississippi" bubbled up to full pressure. In the inky half light, a blond sailor with an oil-blackened face called upon his Norwegian ancestors for aid as he gripped the great steam tap. With a creak, the winch, which had lain at rest for the days that the great black ship had floated at anchor in Uraga Bay, groaned into action. Grunting like a banshee, the sleeping giant of a paddle wheel, began to slowly move. The great iron beam began its upward journey, at its pinnacle, it started to descend. The momentum was transferred down the crankshaft and the paddle wheel moved faster and stronger, churning the deep blue waters into white foaming spray. The gunwales were flecked with foam as the great black war-ship turned full into the outer approaches of Uraga Bay. On the shoreline, the crowds of armed Samurai were still waiting and watching, as they had done for the whole time that Commodore Perry had been at anchor. Slowly and deliberately, the three steam frigates, each with a full-rigger in tow, made for the clear channel and the open sea.

On shore, hands itched to draw swords and to prime matchlocks, but the command to attack did not come. Commodore Perry and his party safely left Japanese territory. To add to the insult, which many felt like a slap in the face, Perry had given an ultimatum that he would return in a year's time and that Japan would open her ports to foreign trade.

As the fleet turned and made for the horizon, the ranks of Samurai sweated quietly, encased in the battle armour in which they had slept for two weeks. The old divisions and feuds which had been suppressed for two hundred and fifty years began to re-emerge. The strain of waiting became too great for some of the

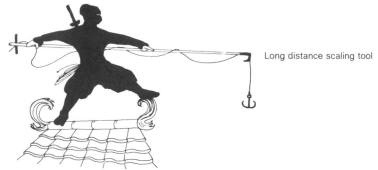

Long distance scaling tool

lower Samurai — amongst the stubble fields all along the road from Edo to Uraga Bay, the dried yellow grass was flecked with blood as new-born "Samurai" tried to prove themselves worthy of their heritage.

One such instance, which serves to illustrate the feeling of the time, took place at the road side, seven ri from the Yokohama side of Kanagawa. Two Samurai of equal rank were walking towards one another, each intent on completing his task of work. They stood at last, eyeball to eyeball, the armour of one dazzling the other.

"Let me pass, I am on the Shōgun's business" said Abe Tetsu taro, aged fifty one years.

"Nay, sir, I have precedence. I am on the Emperor's business," replied one Sugasawa Anjiro aged forty-six years. (His actual "business" was to look for a suitable latrine area for his corps of musketeers).

"Stand back sir," Abe responded, "I will not ask again."

"Over my dead body," Sugasawa spat.

Immediately, swords were drawn, Sugasawa adopted the high Jodan No Kamae stance. His style being Sado Ryu. This particular stance seemed very spectacular but a battle-hardened swordsman would have found it amusing. The two duellists had obviously studied only dojo fencing, not battle reality. Now both had adopted the Jodan No Kamae stance, effectively cancelling

Half chigiriki and han bo technique

one another out. However, brought up on weak Kyoto budo, they did not realise the impasse. Simultaneously used in attack, the two swords glided harmlessly off the Watagami shoulder pieces of each other's armour. Unused to the reality of Batto, they hacked at each other — their sword edges clashed noisily, making great gaping rents in the finely forged steel. As the sun beat down upon them, fine spits of blood dripped onto the ground. Had it not been for a Samurai of middle rank riding past, the futile and ineffective duel would have gone on until both were exhausted. So weak was their technique, that ten well trained spearmen could hold off a hundred such as these. Sweaty and bloody, but neither deeply wounded, they decided if not to call it a draw exactly, then both would continue on their separate paths, vowing to meet another day, but secretly thankful to have neither killed nor been killed. It was all very well, to put on armour and a fine sword, but two hundred and fifty years of deliberately ineffective training could not be unlearned overnight. These were the inescapable facts that both Tokugawa Nariaki and Ii Naosuke, though on opposing sides, saw and sought to correct, each in his own way. Ii Naosuke with his Okinawan Te masters and the battle-hardened spearsmen; Tokugawa Nariaki, with his Ninja.

The two sides rattled blades and growled at each other, all through the long hot summer, after the leaf fall and on into winter. By the first month of the New Year, the minor squabbling of the two factions had resulted in a few ineffective assassination attempts.

The first real action of the Sonno Joi supporters under Tokugawa Nariaki, took place on the evening of the thirtieth day of the first month, at the fortified country residence of Inada Koichi. The snow began falling in profusion and forming huge drifts; masking the walls with a soft canopy of white. As the last flickering light was extinguished in the main body of the residence, Inada Koichi put yet another lurid wood-block book aside, snuffed out his own candle and settled down under his silk brocade futon.

Outside, the moon was obscured by a cloud from all around,

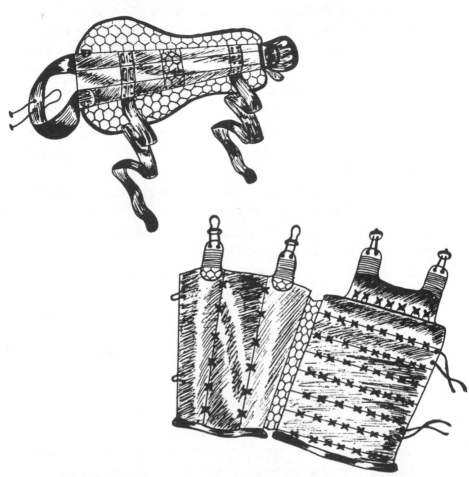

Ninja folding armour

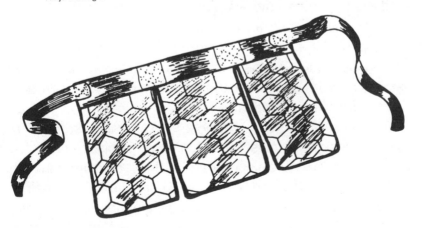

in that strange daylight/dark that a carpet of snow produces, warriors rose out of snow-drifts; clad in ninja combat suits of snow white. They were armed with the familiar musori ninja swords, but this time the handles were wrapped in white silk with the scabbards laquered white. As if responding to an unspoken command, 59 of the white clad ninja moved to the attack. An outer guard, sheltering under a woven straw snow cape, looked slowly round as he heard a faint 'swish'. The white handled naginata cut off his head in one smooth clean action, it bounced on the snow and came to rest upright, looking like a hideous joke, as though someone had taken the trouble to bury him up to his neck. The rest of his body however, fell slowly — spraying the ground in a wide arc as the blood pumped from the artery in the headless neck. Slowly, but with a methodical sureness, the outer defences were overcome. An alert guard did spot the white ninja attack, he reached for the hammer to strike the alarm bell. It was missing, his hands grasped at thin air. The hammer, wielded by Songoro the Dwarf, who was sitting on the bronze bell; slammed down on the guard. He fell silently to the cedar wood floor of the guard tower.

A party of the strongest swordsmen surrounded the house sheltering the Yojimbo body guards. Simultaneously, a party stationed itself outside the room where Inada Koichi was asleep. Moving as one, the parties exploded into action. A few well-placed kicks shattered the wooden amado outer doors. Kenji, a giant of a man, swung an iron Keibo and smashed the Shoji screens behind the amado. White clad ninja poured into the guard's house; anything that moved was cut down in a trice. So great was the carnage, that the white of the ninja suits took on a pink tinge from the tiny spits of blood.

Inside Inada's personal chamber, two Yojimbo sat in seiza, their swords readied for instant action. Two Yari blades exploded out of their chests as two ninja spearmen thrust hard through both wooden amado and wood and paper shoji. The Yari would not come out, so the ninja drew their swords and moved on; leaving the Yojimbo spitted like Yakitori – dead but upright. Inada turned in

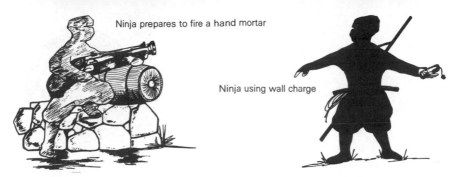

Ninja prepares to fire a hand mortar

Ninja using wall charge

his sleep, the amado close to his face smashed through. There stood Tada Hisamori, leader of the new Tomokatsu Ryu ninja. Inada's eyes opened wide as he saw the wraith-like figure of Tada, clad entirely in white. Struggling from under the heavy weight of the silk and brocade covers, he reached for the ornately decorated sword that rested on an abalone shell laquered Katana Kake sword stand. His hand never got there. Tada's sword flashed once, cutting from right neck to left nipple. The already dead Inada slumped down amongst the covers.

The rout was on. A brief scream from the kitchen area, where the courtesans slept, was silenced as the Kunoichi women ninja cut off their cries with hemp garottes. A Shoji screen slid open and the scribe who Songoro had watched all those months before, rushed out into the arrow covered courtyard, followed by a ninja swordsman. The scribe drew the hidden scroll knife and threw it, hitting the ninja squarely in the chest. It bounced off the under armour and fell harmlessly to the floor. A second later, the scribe's lifeless body followed it.

The entire operation lasted for ten minutes and fourteen seconds. Tada sounded the recall and 59 ninja returned.

"What casualties?" Tada asked the group leaders.

"None sir" came the replies. "Shall we set it to the torch?"

"No!" said Tada. "This must remain as an example. Disperse now. Be back at the castle by moon-rise tomorrow."

At the finish of his words, the crowded scene was empty. Only the wind remained to blow the tattered Shoji screens and creak the shattered amado. In the distance an owl shrieked as the moon came out from behind a cloud, showing for the first time; the horror.

49

the scientific way

"No! No! No!" The corridors of Lord Ii Naosuke's castle rang with the angry cry as the news of the snowy massacre was brought to him. The extent of the atrocity had affected him deeply, stay of execution would not be held back, it would be effected as soon as a horse shod with straw shoes over the iron, could make its way to the temple at Sugiyama. The Okinawans and the spearmen had only been used once since receiving the medallion which gave them absolute authority. That was in a single instance as a show of strength in the right quarters — terrorizing a few of the less powerful village headmen who sympathized with Tokugawa Nariaki. Now Ii Naosuke's hand was drawn.

The black horse, stripped of all that could impede its speed, slithered down the made-up roads and up hills, the incline of which would have defeated a lesser beast. Its flanks became battered and bruised and bloodstained from hitting trees at full tilt as it slid around corners. Finally, in a flurry of snow and ice, the horse came to a stop outside the Sugiyama temple. The messenger beat on the door with the pommel of his long sword.

After a minute, the great door creaked open. The snow from the door fell in large mounds around the messenger, who seemed oblivious to it. From behind the gates appeared the face of a monk

Ninja attack by night

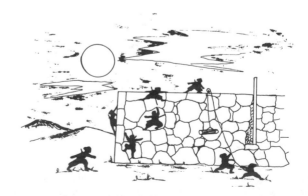

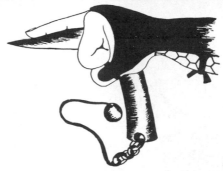

The small Kama

— this time, a genuine monk. The messenger brushed past and down the corridor. Across shiny, polished wood walkways the messenger strode, not bothering to remove the woven straw riding boots. The monk scampered after him, calling the alarm; other monks scurried to clear the way as the messenger padded onwards. Finally, he broke through to the inner compound, as he did so he was surrounded by a hundred yari spears, all pointing directly at him. He could move neither forward nor back.

"I have urgent news from Lord Ii. Let me pass."

The ring of spears did not move. Then the voice of the leader of the Okinawan experts came "Clear a path!" The mercenary spearmen melted back to form a long thin corridor of spears. Unabashed, the messenger strode forward, stopping about two metres in front of the huge Okinawan. Normally he would have adopted Hansonkyo — the bow-low crouch as a mark of respect. But not in this case, for this was an Okinawan and the messenger was a Samurai. He stood tall, as indeed did the mercenary leader, for he was an Okinawan and this was only a Japanese. The two faced eath other.

"You have a message?"

"I speak only to Atosu."

"I am he — speak."

"Lord Ii has ordered me to give you this. Read, or have it read to you."

"Vajra" Fist

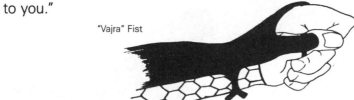

51

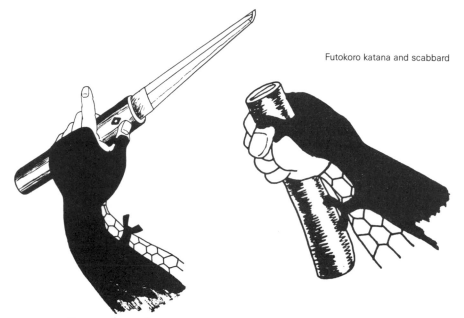

Futokoro katana and scabbard

So saying, the messenger contemptuously brought out an Emaki scroll, he was about to drop it disrespectfully at the Okinawan's feet when his hand shot out, encompassing both the scroll and the messenger's hand.

"Then give it to me" said Atosu as he gripped tighter. The tendons in the messenger's hand stretched and snapped, he did not make a sound but kept staring at Atosu. Atosu released the messenger's hand and unravelled the scroll. He was indeed a man of contradictions, strong as a bull but possessor of an intellect that would easily match one of the Shōgun's advisors. He was a chemist of no mean repute. Coming from a long-oppressed island, where secrecy was a way of life, a whole sub-culture had evolved unknown to the Japanese, who ruled without criticism. Indeed he was the follower of two diametrically opposed ways — the way of China hand and the way of science.

The messenger, bearing a crushed left hand as though it were

By secret stealth the ninja creeps

nothing, turned and walked down the corridor of spears. It was lucky that he had not handled the scroll with his right hand; in the days to come, a man would only be sure of his fate by the power of his sword arm.

Upon leaving the temple, the messenger mounted the black horse and spurred it off down the road. As the horse deftly negotiated an icy patch; the messenger was aware of a strange padding sound becoming louder behind him. He reached for the slung tachi sword at his waist. The padding became louder still. Around the corner ran a young Okinawan, wearing only a fundoshi loin cloth in this extreme cold. The messenger laughed and reined his horse round. The young man, scarcely out of breath, adjusted his pace and halted at about twenty feet away from the messenger.

"Well, Okinawan!" the messenger said.

"You have tried to dishonour Atosu, my master. You will return and apologise."

Hearing these words, the messenger removed his hand from his sword and laughed aloud.

Ha! You are all dogs and your island should be scourged of your kind once and for all."

"Prepare to die," said the young Okinawan.

The messenger laughed again.

"This time filth, you bore me. I think a sharp lesson is in order."

With a flick from the reed horse whip, the messenger urged the horse forward, trying to run the Okinawan down. Instead of running as the messenger had expected, the Okinawan stood his ground. As the horse thundered down upon him, kicking huge clods of snow and frozen earth, the Okinawan uttered a silent spirit-meeting shout as he leapt into the air. His left calloused foot struck the messenger firmly in the stomach, just above the saddle pommel. Using this as a step-hold, the right foot slammed into the messenger's throat. The Okinawan leapt noiselessy down on the other side. The horse reared up, tipping the messenger back off the laquered wooden saddle. He fell back, his head hitting the ground, his body following after. The horse trampled back over the messenger's chest and face, one great hoof crushed his face flat. The horse then sped off down the incline, at great speed, glad to be free of its rider. They say that a horse knows its master's character and in this case, it was indeed so.

The young Okinawan stood and looked briefly at the scene. The messenger was dead, it would appear to have been accidental. He turned and sped back to the secret entrance, before discovery. Soon both spearmen and Okinawans would be called upon in earnest. The plans were set, but the time was not quite right.

Okinawan kama scythe

the last master warrior

Far away from the scenes of murder and political intrigue, in the province of Dewa, lived a family who bore a proud name. In them, the truth that was Samurai life, found expression through the finest flowers of manhood. The name which they bore with pride, in the loyal service of the Oka Clan, was that of Kuroda. The martial tradition which they guarded was one of divine inspiration, known, for want of a better name, as "Spirit of the Wind".

For over two hundred years; ever since Kuroda Hidetaka, son of the Hachiman Samurai, Kuroda Ichitaro, had fought the forces of the evil power invoked by the first Master Tada of the Tomokatsu Ryu Ninja; peace had prevailed. A hard won peace; the result of a fateful encounter of which much has been written and of which I will say no more.

But draw back the private and secret curtain to glimpse a ritual that has passed down the Kuroda family for over two hundred years. Stay silent, for what you will see must be told to no other. The scene is set in the great hall at Oka Castle, the candles flicker. It is the seventh day of the third month. The great hall, constructed of aged wood from the deep, dark forest; grows quiet now. Before the altar, above which is a picture of Kuroda Ichitaro holding a sword and his wife, Shino holding a naginata, sat the elders of the Kuroda. In pride of place sat Kenji, the supreme elder, straight of back and strong of spirit he had seen over 90 winters. He was a magnificent man, not for him, the weak Kyoto Budō. The forces of the Bakufu government had kept a respectful distance throughout the two hundred year history. No Metsuke spy had dared to enter the Kuroda domain.

Kenji, the supreme elder, whose beard was white, sported a full head of white hair. He was immaculately dressed; his eyes

Dutch hour glass – altered for Japanese use

were bright, containing the fire that was the heart of the Wind Spirit. To the young man seated in the middle of the great hall, Kenji was his father's father. It was for Kenji to intone the deep secrets that were the Spirit of the Wind.

It was the young man of 18 summers, Kuroda Ichitaro, he bore the proud name of the Hachiman Samurai, in whose blood coursed the experience of the Bushido though he did not fully realise it.

The great oak clappers, bearing calligraphy of the motto 'Wind Spirit' – 'Spirit Wind', clashed together. The sound resounded through the great hall, flickering the candle flames and disturbing the finely-coiffed hair of Samurai who were to observe the ritual. The time drew nigh; astrologically the right hour came; the sand filled the tiny hour glass at Kenji's left hand side. Having sounded the final resounding clap with the great oak clappers, Kenji carefully placed them at his right hand side and began to speak the secret heart of the initiation ritual. As he did so, there come an unnatural chill, so cold that it felt like a wall surrounding the young Kuroda. Cold beads of icy sweat trickled down his back, but knowing the importance of this mystical moment, for which he had been prepared since his youth, he remained silent and inwardly strove to control his apprehension.

As the supreme edler Kenji's voice swelled in volume, it seemed as if the warriors throughout time who had borne the name Kuroda, were bidden come. Although not physically

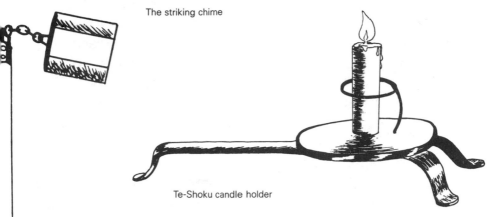

The striking chime

Te-Shoku candle holder

present, they were psychically as real and touchable as one's own skin. Stronger and stronger grew the emotion as the very secrets of nature were unfolded to the Chosen One. As Kenji intoned the depth of the one true secret, an elder removed a long brocade bag of purple and vermillion tied with an ornate Fusa tassle of the finest green silk, from a fine laquer box. Slowly the elder unwrapped the bag to reveal a very old naginata halberd, its handle of fine laquer was chipped with the wear of centuries; that which had once broken had been joined and that which had once been lost had been found.

As the aged Kenji reached a crescendo, the candles in the dark had flickered and gone out. The room was plunged into darkness for an unidentifiable space of time. Then there came a delicate perfume like that of new mown hay and camellias mixed with the resinous smell of the pine forest. As suddenly as they had snuffed out, the candles came alight again, this time burning with a fierce green flame. The faces of the observers took on a ghastly green pallor in the flickering light, this was no light for mortal man. Great shadows flickered against the walls and ceiling of the ancient hall. As Kenji, the supreme elder and guardian of the mysteries of the Wind Spirit, intoned the last word of the secret scroll written on the eve of the carnage of Sekigahara; a gentle wind began to blow. An impossible occurrence, for all the shutters were firmly bolted against prying eyes. Nevertheless, a gentle wind had begun to blow, it increased in intensity until the sleeves of Kimono began to flap like the wings of captive birds. The tightly coiffed hair flew in all directions as the wind buffetted those seated in the hall. Strangely, in all this turmoil, the candles remained upright, their flames apparently untouched by the gale. Slowly the wind subsided, becoming a slight breeze and then it almost imperceptibly faded away. As it faded, the candle flames resumed their normal colour and the great hall returned to a normal temperature. But not everything was the same, there was an unspoken knowing between the young Kuroda and the Supreme Elder Kenji. For a brief moment, time and space had given up their normal bounds, the experience and skill of many lifetimes had crystallised for a brief moment and had set its mark upon the young Kuroda.

Soft tears filled Kenji's eyes as he looked at the young man, but he was happy, the Wind Spirit had manifested itself to a new generation and would continue. Suddenly, the weight of 90 winters grew heavy upon his shoulders, all was as it must be. In must balance Yo, Yin must equate Yang, great power cannot dwell closely in two vessels. With grateful acceptance Kenji started to loosen his ties with life itself. He spoke,

"Kuroda Ichitaro, you bear a proud name and you share a profound secret. I have been spared these 90 years to see this day. Had not your father, my son been taken from us whilst you were still unborn, it would be he who initiates you into the profound mysteries that are the Wind Spirit. Mark well my words. The road you now tread is fraught with danger. The envy of lesser men will always be with you. Do not look at the smiling face, look instead at the smiling heart. Ponder this well —

In my age, I have been granted a brief skill, to understand what has gone before and to see a little of what will yet be. I warn

The great secret scroll of Wind Spirit

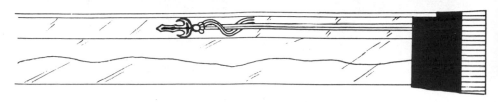

Detail of the Kuroda Sword "Great Liberation"

you, soon Samurai life will be but a memory. The service of generations will count for nothing. A new dawn breaks upon us. Do not be drawn into the conflict too soon. Stand back and observe, let your heart (he used the term Kokoro) guide you. The Wind Spirit will not fail you. When there comes a choice between two pathways, the sign will come if you look with your heart.

Guard this well, for you must be the leader."

With a hand grown suddenly pale, Kenji gestured to the rest of the Kuroda clan who all sat respectfully waiting.

"They know that the depth of the Wind Spirit is not for them, for only the pure blood line can accept this force."

At this, Kenji was silent. He drew his Itomaki No Tachi blade which rested on an ornate single sword stand at his left side. The blade shone with an irridescent glow. With a strange movement, Kenji made a horizontal then two vertical cuts across and right and left of young Kuroda. He then sheathed the sword and held it out for Kuroda who bowed respectfully and took it. He held it horizontally, edge downwards, with the handle to the right. He bowed his head slightly and Kenji returned the bow. From out of his Kimono, Kenji then drew a white Uchiwa fan of sixteen leaves. He opened it with a deft flick revealing a strange poem written on the leaves in Kenji's masterly script, which in its way was an epitaph. With a flinging action, old Kenji threw the fan high into the upper reaches of the great chamber. It spiralled up and then began to fall in the curious way that a fan will, zig zagging like a swallow's tail in summer. As it softly touched the polished wooden floor, the spark left Kenji's eyes and death claimed him. He remained upright in seiza position. There was no feeling of loss, rather a warm happy feeling, felt by all those present. Young Kuroda looked at the fan which had fluttered down near him. He read the poem.

"Like a fan opening and closing
Are we at one with the Spirit
who will carry it on?"

In the realm of the Oka Clan in far away Dewa, a gentle wind began to blow.

Kenji supreme Elder

bloody vengeance

As the red crescent of the sun broke over the crest of skyline, the faded wooden notice board at the entrance of Nihon Bashi bridge; the terminus of all highways leading into the city of Edo; was suffused with a red-gold glow, bringing into sharp contrast the various edicts posted upon it. These were on either red or white paper, depending upon their importance. Shōgonal edicts were written directly onto a wooden board with a special eaved roof, distinguishing the merely banal from what was actually law.

Thus the scene was set and into it came the clatter of a single Jinrikisha. It was pulled by a wizened little man, wearing a fundoshi loin cloth and an indigo blue cotton Happicoat stencil – dyed with the Shō ideogram of his employer. It was from him that the Jinrikisha was rented at an exorbitant rate, the old man also was responsible for all breakages and repairs. Still, even a little life was better than no life at all, so cheerful in adversity, the Jinrikisha man padded on, bearing his Samurai passenger.

From behind the notice board stepped a man dressed in the costume of the watch. He bore the two swords of Samurai rank and a jitte sword breaker which served as the badge of his office. He thrust the jitte forward, pointing it at the Jinrikisha man – "Oh no, not another fine!". As a class, Jinrikisha men were frequently preyed upon by officers of the watch who thus supplemented their income.

The green tassel swayed to and fro from the handle end of the jitte. The Jinrikisha pulled to an abrupt stop. The Samurai passenger who had been dozing quietly, jerked awake. He was thick-headed following a night's "entertainment", at Yoshiwara. Here, incognito, he had drank, gambled and whored the night away. Now, in the light of dawn, he was skulking back to the outer post by the Tokkaido where lay his day's work. He bore the unmistakeable crest that marked him as a Samurai of Tokugawa Nariaki and that was as good as a signed warrant from a magistrate. The drunken Samurai started to rise to his feet, the Jinrikisha driver was picked up and the Jinrikisha tilted back as the balance of weight was shifted.

A su-yari struck the Samurai from behind, followed by a magari-yari coming from his right side. Thus pinioned, the Samurai was lifted out of the Jinrikisha, depositing the driver flat on his backside between the shafts of the vehicle. He winced, expecting a sword to strike him, but no attack came. Instead, the man dressed as an officer of the watch, placed the jitte to one side and from the fold of his Kimono, produced a 10 rin gold weight. This he tossed to the driver, placed one finger over his lips and indicated that it would be better if the Jinrikisha was not there. Seizing what for him was a small fortune, the driver padded off as quickly as he could, the Jinrikisha bouncing and clattering as he made his escape. The drunken Samurai was now the dead Samurai, after the two spears had picked him from the vehicle, another ten had made sure that there was no mistake. All over Edo, at that precise moment, followers of Tokugawa Nariaki were meeting similar fates. In total, forty one, the exact number of those massacred at Inada's headquarters.

However the revenge was not yet complete for the murdered Samurai were only of low to middle rank, a figure head of greater standing was needed — one had been chosen, the owner of the secret Kura storehouse, Sasano. Murderer of the Kunoichi ninja and a man marked by Tada.

Relying solely upon their intelligence network; at the same time as the various low ranking Samurai felt the cold edge of steel; a party of Okinawans, dressed in fireman's uniform carrying bamboo ladders and climbing poles, burst through the outer defences of Sasano's headquarters. With a few well-placed firebombs on the outer buildings and cries of "Fire!" on their lips, the confusion caused was enough for them to bluff their way to the inner moat where Sasano's underground headquarters lay. Using

the ladders and climbing poles as makeshift bridges, they crossed en masse to the central man-made island. The drawbridge was up, so pulling their ladders and poles after them, they were assured of an undisturbed action.

With a mighty thud, the Kura storehouse doors flew open. A party of ten Samurai guards, swords drawn, dashed out. They quickly fanned out in a semi-circle around the entrance and ropes pulled the great doors closed. Seizing the initiative, two of the Okinawans drew the razor sharp long handled Kama scythes. Almost without thinking, they aimed and threw. The Kama whirled over the heads of the defending Samurai and landed to cleanly cut the ropes. The heavy doors stopped half open. Two long poles were thrust through in an X formation with two stocky Okinawans grimly holding them open. Hands inside, realising that their fortress was vulnerable, hacked and tore at the poles. The semi-circle broke as those Samurai too tried to cut at the poles. This break was enough. A party of two Okinawans leapt up and over the cross of poles, nunchaku rice flails spinning in deadly arcs, they cut down anything that moved at the top of the dark stairs which led to Sasano.

One of the Okinawans holding the poles had been cut by a swordsman. A long gash ran down his left arm. Leaving the pole in the care of an able replacement, he let out an ear-piercing yell and leaped at the swordsman who had attacked him. The swordsman made a vital error — he assumed that the unarmed man was not armed — but as a secret Okinawan study motto states,

"Behold the empty hand
Edged with the truth hard won
Becomes a sword in righteousness."

The swordsman's last living recollection was of a very large fist swinging towards his head. Thus, by contemptuously underestimating the opposition, did all the line of Samurai die. To clear the way, their bodies were thrown over the edge of the dry moat where they remained as a gristly set piece.

Two abreast, the Okinawans charged down the steps, rapidly blinking to make the dark become light. As they became accus-

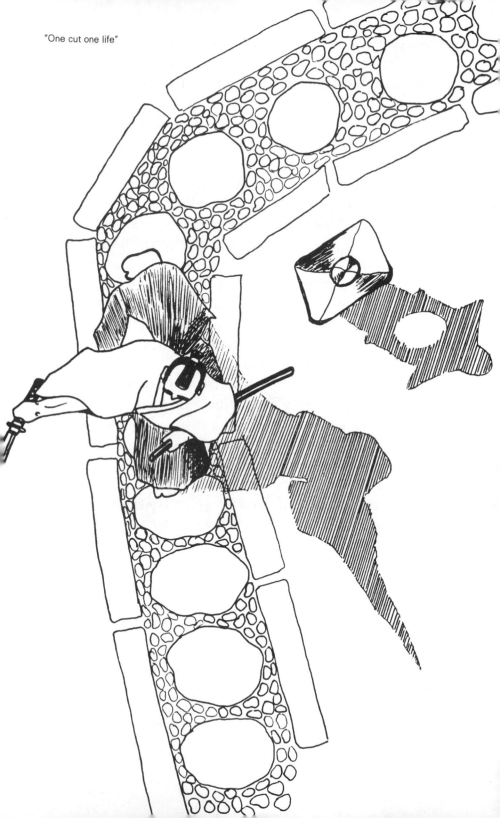

"One cut one life"

tomed to the darkness, they were able to see the length of the corridor facing them. In the distance the defending Samurai were hastily assembling the prototype rapid firing gun. Not knowing exactly what it could be, except that it was not an invitation to take tea, the Okinawans rushed head long at it. A Samurai pulled and pulled at the firing mechanism, the breech block dropped, trapping the loader's hands. The feed magazine fell to the floor, spreading rolled paper percussion tubes over the floor, some ignited but were just like firecrackers. A Samurai drew one of the Colt pistols and aimed it, but a flying reverse roundhouse to the calf felled him. This was followed by a stamping kick to the throat and the Samurai was no more. Abruptly an earthenware flask of oil was thrown around a corner, followed by a flaming torch. Because of his quick reactions, one of the leading Okinawans caught it with a namigaeshi returning wave kick on the sole of his foot. He flicked it up to chest height where his two powerful, calloused hands snuffed the life out of the flame. The passage-way was soon littered with the bodies of fallen Samurai. Apart from the two Kama scythes and the nunchaku rice flails, the Okinawans had not resorted to their own arsenal of weapons; almost as though they had contempt for the fine-forged swords of the Samurai — to the Okinawans, they represented two hundred years of suppression.

The cold grey stones of the underground redoubt took on the appearance of a crypt as more than twenty Samurai dead littered the edges. As the bold party of Okinawans burst through the end of the corridor, they came into the treasure store. The fine laquered armours and ceramics stored in paulownia wood boxes held no aura of mystery for them. They could have been filled with dust for all the Okinawans cared. What of gold? That might be a different tale, but victory was the main prize now. At the end of the treasure hall was the inner sanctum. Its entrance was stoutly bolted with two inch thick boards of fine oak, bound with iron bands, pierced with metal studs. In the dead centre of this barri-cade was a single port-hole, like a hideous eye.

The Okinawan party wanted to rush headlong at this stout

Sword and iron fan

door, but Atosu their leader, held them back. His knowledge of chemistry was more than a match for this last ditch defence by Sasano. As an experiment to test the field of fire, Atosu drew a long handled sleeve entangler from the rack which held it horizontally on the wall. Its finely laquered shaft was inset with tiny spirals of sea shells, which had been polished flat and let into the dark, lustrous urushi laquer surface.

Seizing a red laquered mempo face mast and helmet from one of the armour stands, he proceeded to tie both mempo and helmet to the crosspiece end of the sleeve entangler. The steel spike projections of the entangler made a fine key for the brocade lined hemp tieing cords. With this strange "doll's head" atop the weapon, the leader pushed it out over the top of the finely chisseled line of store boxes in rapid succession, five shots from Sasano't model 1847 Colt pistol rang out. The leader then moved the decoy back behind the boxes, to appear an instant later at the other side. Two more shots rang out as Sasano struggled to control the blind panic that overtook him. He was alone, locked up in the bowels of the earth, sixteen feet thick stone walls surrounded him as he awaited his fate. In each hand he held a hastily primed Colt pistol, forced out of the last box which Sasano had not "disposed of". Black powder and percussion caps littered the square flag-stone floor as he rushed to save himself.

Twenty minutes later, Atosu, the Okinawan leader had discovered the blind spot in Sasano's spy hole. One by one, laquer boxes, containing fine armours, ceramics and scrolls were moved to block the door. The occasional shot rang out, as Sasano fired at someone he thought he had seen, but he was firing only at a cloth playfully shaken here and there, to draw his fire whilst his fellows busied themselves at the door. With a final shove, the last box was in place.

An Okinawan was ordered outside to get some soil, a fine laquered fifty six plate suji bachi helmet was tossed to him to serve as a bucket. Atosu then busied himself with a vial of green/brown liquid. This he carefully mixed with the reddish powdered contents of a metal bottle. He carefully rocked the mixture from

Kama vs yari

Sai vs keibo

side to side as the chemical reaction took place. The resultant yellowish paste settled into the small bamboo tube which had been constructed for it. With a few leaves of paper torn from a record box, this tube was wedged in the centre of a crack between two of the beams. The Okinawan, returning with the soil, was surprised to be told to make water in it. He laughed and cheerfully urinated into the soil, only to cry out a few seconds later as the excess percolated through the soil to the tehen hole at the top of the helmet and thence over his sandalled feet. But behind this comedy there was a deadly earnest reason. The mud paste thus produced in the helmet was forced over the bamboo tube of chemical. The helmet was then propped tightly to the door with boxes and brocades until the whole of the door was draped and swathed with boxed and hangings. The Okinawan leader beckoned all of his followers back into the safety of the corridor where he bid them sit down and wait. Ten minutes elapsed, then from the treasure store there came a loud "pop!" – not a bang. At that the leader was up and tearing away the boxes from the door. As he did so, the smell of sulphurous smoke and burning flesh filled the air. The compound mixed by the leader, had completed its reaction and exploded. As the force was contained within the mud and iron bowl, it went the other way, blasting a gaping hole in the oak beams and an even bigger hole in Sasano who had crouched behind the door like a scared mouse. The gunpowder had exploded, creating even more havoc, thus when the tattered door was forced open, almost nothing remained – except pieces of twisted metal and slowly smoking flesh.

The deed was done. Atosu ordered his men out, with enough gold for the whole party, including the spearmen who were not to be crossed. The party of Okinawans scattered across roof tops and over walls, as pre-arranged fires burst out all over Edo.

Sadly, what no one yet realised was that of the two opposing sides; Tada and his Ninja and Atosu and his Okinawans and spearmen, the command structures had been severed. Both the offices of Ii Naosuke and Tokugawa Nariaki, disavowed any knowledge of the perpetrators of the two outrages. Like mad dogs set loose amongst sheep, only disaster could follow.

the token of peace

Masterless, the ninja under Tada's command, had been driven out of their castle stronghold in Koga province; true to form, they had melted away to other careers and lives which had been planned for them.

The temple at Sugiyama was conveniently burnt to the ground in a "lightning storm". Strange that summer lightning should come from a cloudless sky. The Okinawans had taken to the hills and the spearmen had run off to the nearest seaport. Here they sold their lives bloodily to hijack one of the Shōgun's ships. With their numbers reduced to a half of their former strength, they struck out for what they thought to be the Korean coast, where they hoped to make passage for China and a warlord in search of mercenary help.

At fighting and killing, they may have been expert, but at seamanship and navigation they were singularly inept. After forty six days afloat, starved and half crazy, they were blown out of the water by a British frigate, patrolling the opium route near Shanghai.

Things could not have looked blacker. That next summer, the Kurafune black ships returned and Commodore Perry had his treaty. As the year progressed, the area of the Yokohama began to

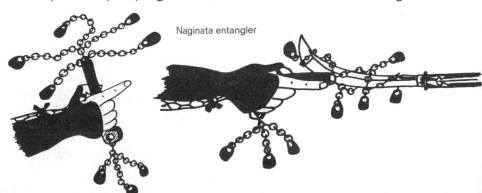

Naginata entangler

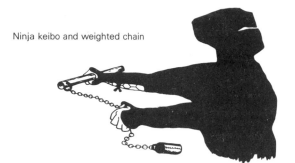

Ninja keibo and weighted chain

be dug up and re-claimed from the sea. As the months passed into years, the tall "blond hairs" walked the highways and byways. Then strange and unexplained murders of a number of foreigners began to occur. Some were the result of actual bad behaviour on the foreigner's part, but more than a few had no rational explanation. None, that is, unless you were privy to the developing intelligence network which was growing between the foreigners and the Japanese who were in their pay. "Japanners" as the foreigners called them, began to adopt Western dress and modes of living. Indeed it was most strange to see a man wearing thick wooden geta, stovepipe trousers, a frock coat, shirt and cravat, with the daisho long and short swords thrust through his sash. His head shaved with a chomage oiled top knot. Some even carried bearskin top hats, which they could not wear because of the top knot, but which they brandished much in the manner of a fan in social matters. The whole ensemble was very strange and indeed had not gone unnoticed by those who mattered. Many men were marked for death — which arrived swiftly — by the sword.

By a strange, or perhaps not so strange, coincidence, those other foreigners, the Okinawans who had "gone to ground" in the woods, perfectly at one with nature, had been satirized by the populace. There was even a burlesque play portraying them as bumbling dolts, falling over and farting, to the great amusement of villagers. But they do say that one fears most what one makes fun of. The Okinawans were totally unmoved by such ridicule, choosing instead to double their training programme. Soon, in many highland areas, it was possible to stumble upon a clearing hacked out of virgin forest. To find also, rudimentary punching posts worn smooth by many powerhouse strikes with calloused

Yari spear with wrapped bamboo leaf laquered scabbard

hands. No indication of where or why the Okinawans had gone, could ever be found for they covered their tracks with a skill rivalling that of the ninja. And what of the ninja? They as always, slept, awaiting the call to arms.

Tada, however, did not sleep. He was active in the background, observing and planning, waiting until the right moment came. Come it did, in the Spring of 1862. News filtered through, first secretly and then in greater profusion, of the war that was raging in America. Old wounds ached in the castles up and down Japan. The Kensai sword saint, Musashi, had said in his last testament, that timing was all in strategy – a timing in both the flourishing and the downfall of all things.

Secretly the old clans began to strengthen their ties, albeit in secret. A plan emerged to once and for all rid Japan of the barbarian scourge. A fantastically elaborate plan of assassinations of both governments and royalty throughout Europe was evolved. It was scheduled to begin with the assassination of the American President on American soil. Protocol demanded that the only method of death available was the sword. Of course, such proposals were impossible but proud men facing the anihilation of a thousand years' strong way of life almost overnight, reacted in less than logical ways. Firmly convinced of the power of Yamato Damashi, the warrior spirit at the fountain head of Samurai ideals their plans did not seem stupid nor impossible.

A band of twenty two young Samurai was mustered and under the pretence of a cultural exchange, they set sail from the newly-constructed harbour at the Yokohama — a few short weeks later their craft dropped anchor in San Francisco. They disembarked, firmly imagining that the President lived in San Francisco. They tied their sleeves up in true Samurai fashion, hitched up their brocade hakama, drew their swords and charged off down the Du Pont Gai, looking for the President's "palace". After a few encounters with the dockside community, "the crazy Chinese men" as they were dubbed by the locals, were isolated by the militia, at the worm-eaten end of a bonded pier. Realising that escape was impossible, the party of fanatics turned their swords upon themselves and in the manner of their forbears, committed Seppuku. For the curious; the souvenir hunters, the fine blades made interesting acquisitions. The newly ensconced ambassador from Japan was summoned. Amidst threat and counter-threat, the whole incident was covered up with a wrapping of "strong red tape".

Back in Japan, the apprentice War Lords were crestfallen and in true Samurai fashion began to fight amongst themselves. Sensing the moment, Tada, master of the Tomokatsu Ryu Ninja, sent out the secret call. From highways and byeways; out of the dark shadows, the ninja materialised. They formed into four groups of twenty five — each totally self sufficient. Skilfully, and for the highest reward possible, Tada "played off" warlord against warlord, arranging for all four groups to work at once. One simple rule only applied — destroy anything that was not ninja. Thus the cycle of carnage was spurred into action. The warlords were pleased with their petty victories and after each raid upon outlying guard posts or the liberation of a grain store, Tada was called upon to put matters to right. Not once did anyone suspect that Tada was "playing one off against the other". All the time, Tada was getting closer to Dewa Province. With the unrest that was sweeping the suburban lands, the wily band of Okinawans was driven further and further inland. They despaired of ever seeing the sea or tasting its salt spray again. To an island race, this was the bitterest of blows. Yet they doubled their resolve and continued to inhabit the wild places, continued their deep practice of the pro-

A Samurai shows off his new clothes from the Yoko Hama

A Samurai adapts to Western fashion

found mysteries of hand and foot. Often, when the half-light of dawn grew chill did a thought return of far away Okinawa, their lands and their families. Their leader knew these thoughts well and he tried, as well as he could, to stir up a fervour for training — as the Okinawan training maxim said —

> "My home is nought
> By hands and feet be wrought,
> And thus in depth, our spirit caught."

But in all truth, there is a limit to the capacity of man's enduring, beyond which a mortal dare not go. In the deep studies of the mystery, there is a point which transcends both the physical and the spiritual, it is in truth, a purity of essence. A Sennin by another name. But those who have journeyed fully down its rocky path have not returned and many, too many, died or simply became mad. The leader was aware of all this. In his hands was the responsibility for not just the men under his command but also a responsibility to those who waited at home in Okinawa.

Bronze and ivory sculpture by Ogata, given to U.S. Ambassador

An inro pill box with star of Perry design

many rivers to cross

Four years after the time that the Ambassador to Japan from America, Townsend Harris, had beaten down the waves of prejudice and weathered the savage murder of his personal aide Henry Heusken, he was finally granted the honour of an audience with the Shōgun, Iesada, in Edo. Not knowing what to do, regarding protocol, the Shōgun was sitting on seven tatami mats to elevate his position over the barbarian giant – Harris, for his part was concerned not to appear in public barefoot. To this end, he changed in a new pair of shoes at the edge of the brocade-bordered tatami mats. The protocol of centuries was broken by the barbarian who wore shoes indoors in the Shōgun's presence. Had not the self control of the Lord's been paramount, Harris would have been cut down where he stood. But even with this act, the Samurai knew that the evil could not be thrust away, soon Samurai life would count for nothing, except in the heart of those who kept its real secrets.

The guardian of one such secret, that known as the Spirit of the Wind, had grown to manhood, and as retainer of the Oka clan in far away Dewa province, was not unduly concerned with the events in Edo. Throughout its history, the Oka and their retainers, the Kuroda, had not been overly affected by the great changes throughout the centuries, they tried to remain untouched by the weakness of fashion. In its unperturbable heart, the Kuroda were the spiritual overseers of the area.

In a forest glade, a hawk loosed from the gloved hand of its master soared high and then struck its quarry like lightning. Killing quick and killing clean, the hawk sprang up into the sky. Higher and higher, soaring and diving then hovering as it enjoyed the pure ecstasy of its own existence. At one with the element, its blood

Samurai assassins roam the land

coursed hot and powerful through its veins, envigorating the very root tips of its wing feathers which gave it flight. All movement was registered by its sharp eyes, its head flicked to and fro — from its master, on his fine white stallion, so far below, to the movement of a young deer deep in the forest canopy. Then not seen, but felt, truly felt, "must go, my master, must return, danger — strange". The hawk faltered and returned to the outstretched glove. Kuroda — he slipped the hood of fine soft leather over the bird's head. He knew that something was amiss. He did not feel danger for himself, he probed the great emptiness with the subtle technique known as "returning echo". As the heir to the Wind

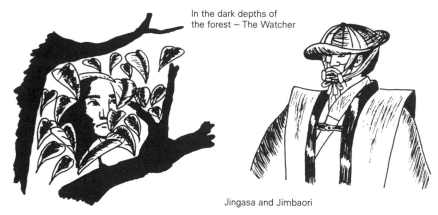

In the dark depths of the forest — The Watcher

Jingasa and Jimbaori

Spirit, he held power greater than his years would suggest. His normally restless white stallion, the pride of the Oka stables, was strangely subdued as it felt the awesome power of the Wind Spirit. Kuroda closed his eyes, so that only a faint slit of light filtered through, merging grey with the forest green. He felt a presence near, at his left side. It was a watching presence, not malicious, several different emotions with one single will. One leader and several followers — far away. Almost too far. Kuroda concentrated, extending his circle of awareness like the ripples on the calm surface of water after a stone is thrown. Far away, he sensed many, over twenty separate emotions. But a crystallisation held by one all-encompassing feeling (the rest of the Okinawans were engaged in training far away in a forest glade).

A wry smile crossed Kuroda's lips as he felt a prickling sensation at the back of his neck causing the small hairs in his otherwise perfectly-dressed hair to stand on end. He himself was being probed; the power was far more direct, strong; but against the Wind Spirit, crude in comparison. Kuroda turned his face in the direction of the prober. The dark depth of the forest yawned green and gaping, defying all but the bravest to dare to enter. But as the Wind Spirit leads, so a man must follow. Kuroda pressed with his knees and the fine white stallion began to slowly move forward. As he waited for his eyes to accustom to the dark greens and browns of the verdant forest, he probed with the occult side of the Wind Spirit. He felt the same single, strong spirit, coupled with other less strong spirits. But even these were more resolute in their depths than any that Kuroda had encountered before. Although unknown, Kuroda did not feel any danger. He loosened the ties on his jingasa laquered helmet. He brushed the side of his jimbaori over-coat to cover the hilt of his finely mounted tachi — mounted in the Ito Maki style whereby half of the scabbard is cross-wrapped in the same manner as the handle with dark green silk braid over samé ray skin; the old hunting style. Here in Dewa Province, things did not change quickly, simply for the sake of fashion. By thus covering the handle of his tachi, Kuroda symbolically demonstrated that although armed, he did not have aggressive intent.

The proud white horse trotted majestically, deeper into the forest. Carefully it trod out the path of least resistance. As it stepped and side-stepped over fallen trees and past rocks and pot-holes, Kuroda became strongly aware of the overpowering closeness of his watchers. He gently reined in the horse, which obediently stopped, shieing slightly. Kuroda's hand smoothed the silky white mane that had been ornately cross plaited, the horse quietened, feeling the calmness of its master.

Kuroda dismounted and spying a large boulder, weathered smooth and green with moss, he led the white horse to its side. Carefully, deftly, he squatted on top of the granite boulder and proceeded to remove his jingasa. As he carefully untied the three silk brocade ties which bound the laquered helmet to his head, he

became aware of a number of presences, which circled, intertwining, behind him. A slight smile crossed his lips as he realised
that he was being tested. As the final tie was loosed, he pulled the
jingasa forward and off, briefly covering his face. In doing so, he
felt one of the presences launch an attack to his back. Using the
full force of his training, Kuroda leaped straight up at the exact
moment that a huge foot swung at him. But the foot kicked only
air. The owner of the massive foot gasped, never had he missed
before. He was still bemused as Kuroda lightly landed behind him.
Sensing his target, the Okinawan turned and launched another
attack. Another time, another place and Kuroda's sword would
have spoken bitter words of death. But not today – this was fun! A
second Okinawan entered the fray and launched a jumping
double fist strike to Kuroda's chest. Flicking his hips, the powerhouse punches, met air, then with a "rat tat", Kuroda struck both of
the Okinawans with the jingasa in quick succession, not to wound
or injure, just to show that if he wished, he could strike them
down. Kuroda resumed his throne atop the granite boulder. The
two Okinawans looked at each other, then into the depths of the
forest where the watcher waited. One of them crossed his eyes
briefly as a silent message, then the two men leaped forward to
land heavily on the mossy top of the boulder. They slithered on the
oily surface; Kuroda simply stood on one leg, balancing himself,
as the two giants fell from the boulder as rain water slides off a
roof.

"Enough!" came the booming voice of Atosu.

The two Okinawans melted back to the safety of the forest.
Kuroda remembered the protocol of the situation and sat in the
dignified Tate Hiza, the only way for a gentleman to sit. There
came a rustling of leaves, the branches parted and there stood
Atosu. He was clad in a simple brown Kimono with breech
hakama in dark blue and soft straw sandals. Thrust through his
sash was a curious-looking affair – part sai, part chain chigiriki. It
was a weapon of his own devising – in his hands, a deadly
whirling terror. But now his hands hung loosely at his sides, their
calloused skin shone irridescent white.

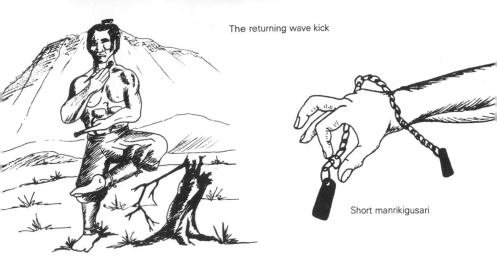

The returning wave kick

Short manrikigusari

Kuroda looked at Atosu. With the depth of the Wind Spirit he knew that which was beyond knowing and saw that which was beyond seeing. In a forest glade in far away Dewa, Kuroda Ichitaro, Samurai retainer of the Oka clan, master of the secret sword and body art of the Wind Spirit, performed something which no Samurai had done nor, under pain of death, would do. He faced Atosu and bowed.

Atosu was visibly shaken but he returned the bow. His supporters gasped as they witnessed the unthinkable. The two warrior masters faced each other across the forest glade, their racial and cultural differences put aside. They were both warriors, seekers after truth by the warrior way and that was the true mark of a man. By nothing else could his merit be judged if not by his resolute acceptance of death. After a moment that defied time, Kuroda broke the silence —

"You have need."

Atosu remained silent, he was advanced in the deep way, but the depth of the Wind Spirit frightened him. Kuroda quickly realised his over-zealousness.

"Forgive me, my friend. I enquire too deeply and without formal right. I am Kuroda Ichitaro, Samurai retainer of the Oka clan. I am a warrior pilgrim of the deep mystery. I bear neither you nor your party any ill will. I recognise you to also be a warrior pilgrim. I humbly request that you consider yourself the guest of the Oka clan on whose land you now stand."

Kuroda then bowed slightly again and remained silent. A few minutes passed, as a pigeon fluttered through the trees, causing the hunting bird tethered to Kuroda's saddle to flutter its wing feathers, Atosu cleared his throat and in a deep Okinawan voice began to speak.

"I am Atosu Anko, master of the Te. I am a mercenary from the islands known as Ryu Kyu."

It was a typical speech, short, precise, not a word wasted.

"Greetings Atosu." Kuroda replied. "Now I must repeat myself for I am given the power to see and say that which is beyond normal sight. You have need?"

Kongo Sai with unusual Itomaki
No Katate wrapping

"Yes" said Atosu, "great need."

"Well," continued Kuroda, "I will not ask why you are here in Japan, for as long as you do not threaten my land of Oka, your business is your own."

Atosu thought, then, drawing himself up straight, replied.

"My party and I, along with a group of murdering spearmen, for which I have no respect, were contracted to work for a certain Lord. I will not compromise you by revealing his name, suffice it to say, that it is foremost in the land."

"I see" said Kuroda diplomatically.

"But," continued Atosu, "fates were against us and Tada's ninja robbed us of our patron, so here we are, with nowhere else to go."

Iron tonfa

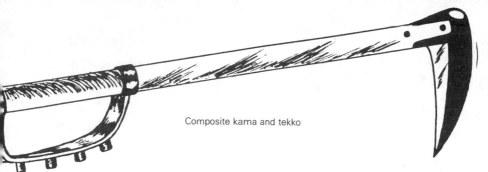

Composite kama and tekko

At the mention of Tada's name, a cold shock of seven generations ran down Kuroda's spine.

"So" he mused, "the battle is joined again."

Atosu looked puzzled. Kuroda regained his composure.

"Excuse me" he said "but the name of which you speak is known to me. It is a name which I thought had died out over two centuries ago."

Atosu remained silent. Kuroda continued.

"For your safety, I will show you the place where no-one goes. It is my own training ground. You may rest there until it is right for you to go. I have a store of provisions hidden there, so you will not want for food."

Atosu looked closely at Kuroda. True, he was a hated Samurai, a member of the class that had held his forbears in slavery for centuries. But there was something different about this man — a

Talon kama

natural honesty and great power emanated from him. Atosu decided to trust him. He waved first his left, then his right arm in a slow deliberate arc — the watchers came out of the shadows — they stepped unsurely. Atosu dispatched a runner to fetch the rest of the party and soon the glade was filled with Okinawans. Atosu leaped onto the boulder next to Kuroda. He scanned the faces; he was a good commander and he knew the hearts of his followers.

"My friends, I say we trust him."

Once again, short and to the point, and the men accepted it. Atosu was their leader and he had never let them down.

dark and dreadful

Far across the corridors of memory and down the passages of time, the elementals craved life again.

In the flickering halo of an oil lamp, a single figure sat hunched against the icy cold in the precinct of a ruined mill. The great studded wooden paddle wheel stood useless; wanting for water which had been diverted a century or more ago, what use is a mill that will not work. So, amidst the dust of a hundred summers, sat Tada, Ninja of the Tomokatsu Ryu. His hands trembled slightly as he held the box of boxes. Locked away for over two centuries, it contained vileness and horror. With bony fingers, he broke the wax seals which his forbear had set on them. As the final seal split, Tada placed the small box on a low shelf in front of him. He pulled out a square of purple silk and dusted the top of the stone ground ishime laquer; set into the box, in a curious script, was the message of power –

"Set in blood, will closed be

Set in blood, will open be."

Stealing his nerves, Tada drew his aikuchi tanto dagger. The heavy blade shone in the lamp's flicker, casting shadows of dark imaginings all around the mill-yard. Holding the tanto in his right hand, Tada opened his left and spread his fingers wide. He lay the edge of the tanto across the line which ran from the base of his index finger, to the centre of his wrist and intoning the words –

"Power beyond belief,

Evil beyond belief."

He dragged the blade across the palm of his hand. The well-forged blade cut deeply, drinking up the life blood as it cut a bone-deep swathe in Tada's hand. Rasping curiously, it sounded as though someone was tearing fine material. The blood dripped

Ninja with short shaft naginata and lead ring

onto the top of the box, which seemed to soak it up like a sponge, leaving no trace nor stain on the surface. Tada felt suddenly weak and a thought crossed his mind that he was actually going to die, as though somehow, the demon box was soaking the very life out of him. The tanto fell noisily to the flagstones of the mill-yeard. With his good right hand he grasped the box, his fingers tightened around it and he lifted it up. His left hand seemed welded above the lid as the blood poured relentlessly, in pulsating rhythms on to the box, only to disappear and then be replaced by the increasing flow.

What was left of any human dignity within Tada's mind, struggled hard to gain the strength to throw the vile box away into the mill race — anywhere to be rid of its all pervading evil. But the madness was out, forces had been called up, the elementals would be satisfied. A life for a life and a soul for a soul, that was the rule, as the first Tada had discovered over two centuries before. Those who called up the great force must be prepared to pay its price — in full. Tada's eyes bulged as his whole mind was racked

The deadly over the shoulder sword draw

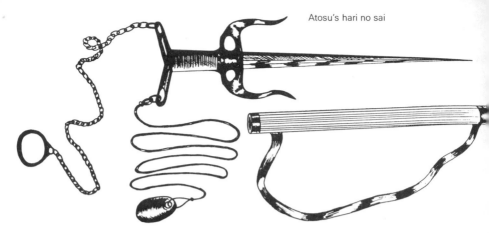

with pain beyond belief. He put the box back onto the shelf. His right hand smoked slightly as though it were charred — still his left hand hovered, spreading red and wet.

"Help me!!" screamed his tortured mind.

But it was too late, the cry of pain was not transferred to his lips. It bounced about inside his head like a dull hammer beat, resounding back and forth, left and right. Icy cold sweat glistened on Tada's forehead and rivulets of it poured down his back. Then the shaking started, maybe the ground was shaking as well, or perhaps it was just Tada caught in the grasp of a malevolent hand. He shook faster and faster until his head became a blurred image .

Purple smoke began to rise from the gaps between the flagstones, enveloping Tada's body like a shroud. A low moan began to rumble from the very depths of the earth, gathering in speed and pitch until it became a screaming whine. Then, through bloodshot eyes, Tada saw the box. Huge cracks appeared in the laquered surface as if something were trying to break out, like an egg close to hatching. From far away, a metallic drumming started to beat; louder and louder, matching in volume and intensity, the screaming whine. Then, as if a plug had been pulled, the sound stopped. The silence was tangible, just as oppressive and twice as evil.

Tada's body shook once, then twice. He fell forward onto the laquered box which shattered like crisp pastry. There was a strange, sweet smell of cloves and lemon balm. Mercifully a great blackness came over Tada like a blanket and all was silence.

The deep blue of dawn light drove the stars away. In the mill-yard all was grey. The figure of Tada was huddled where he had fallen, his Kimono and hakama glistened with silver droplets of dew. Then as orange and red streaked the dawn sky, Tada stirred. Like a child awakening from a deep slumber, he rose wiping the sleep from his eyes. He sat up and incredulously looked down. The box was just a pile of brown powder. He looked at his hand, the cut that should be bone deep, had completely healed. Only a thin white scar remained to attest that the events of the previous evening had indeed happened. All that remained — except for his eyes, there was something strange about them which could not be defined. Was it just a look, or something age old? The sign of the elemental was about him, he was marked as a man apart.

Knives by moonlight

Now Tada began to piece together the events of the previous evening, no memory was barred to him, all was open. Then a strange thing happened, almost accidental, almost intended — Tada thought of the great castle where he had so recently been governor. He felt himself transported there, at first the images were shaky and indistinct and then gradually they became stronger. Slowly Tada realised that he was not seeing recollected images of the past, but pictures of the present. The ninja lore was right — it said that whoever had the courage to break the seals on the box would accrue powers of untold number.

Tada looked about him in wonder. High on an outcrop of weathered stone, a bird sat, greeting the dawn with a plaintive cry. Tada channelled his energies and pointed with his index finger at the small bird. He then shouted. His Kiai echoed around the ruined buildings. The tiny bird fell spinning and twisting until it hit the ground and lay still.

"Good, very good" Tada whispered to himself, he chuckled with a demonic laugh, then checked himself. It was as though something or someone else was laughing inside him, but he paid it no heed. Instead, he chose to channel his energy to wondering whether the Kiai would drop a man, only time would tell. Tada rose, brushed himself down and moved to a low papapet wall. He sat down on it and thought deeply for a few moments. Then all became clear, so simple — when all changes, you must change. Soon Japan would be a modern nation with an army of conscripts, a Navy and who could tell what else. The old ways of ninja life

must be remembered, but the new ways must be explored. Best leave the rest of the new ninja sleeping a while longer, until the lay of the land became clearer.

Tada turned inwards to himself. He said the word, "Edo, Edo", soon in his mind's eye, he was there. Everything looked slightly blurred but he was able to discern the Shōgun's residence and the brash buildings that were being constructed in "modern" style. Wires were being strung from the lofty branches of the trees along the Tokkaido, as the "talking wire" was set up. Tada delved deep – in a womb-like warmth which pervaded his very being, he saw what was and what might yet be. In his mind's eye, he saw a great army of Japanese, dressed in the European manner. They carried the modern Martini-Henry carbine and mortars of French manufacture. Behind them snorted and puffed a great iron monster. Its heart was flame and its breath like the steam of Beppu. The very earth shuddered as the great wheels holding the monster to its two iron strips, began to turn. Tada's attention moved again, deeper and deeper. The wells of memory were drained; past and future became as one. Far away in space and time, on a mountain known as Shiroyama, the final conflict between a peasant army and the forces of Samurai virtue, led by Saigo Takamori, paid heavily in blood for the price of progress. But out of defeat, are sown the seeds of victory and Tada's mind became filled with images of the new era; too much for his frame to bear. Merciful blackness. When he recovered again, the day had passed as swiftly as a candle is snuffed out and stars pricked the night sky.

Tada opened his eyes. He was looking upwards and two identical pictures of the universe filled his mind, he blinked, once, twice, and the images merged into one. The star field twinkled brightly. Near the big dipper, a red star burnt like a hot coal, becoming brighter and brighter until it filled Tada's view. A rushing sound, like the inside of a whirlpool when the spring rains flood to the sea, filled the air of the mill-yard. This occult moment of moments branded, in an instant, an area that would come to fruition a hundred years on, but leave that for another tale.

"Remember this, I am he who cries in the wilderness. Two centuries separate us. You bear the proud name of Tada, you are of my seed....."

Tada shook his head to clear it of this nonsense, but it would not be driven away. Slowly, insidiously, like some vile fever, the presence had grown within Tada. From the moment that the seals on the box had been broken, Tada's soul was on sale to the highest bidder and the price was 'knocked down' to one of his own ancestors.

Chain spike

Over two hundred years before, a Tada Ninja Master had paid the ultimate price and had condemned his soul to wander the night without rest nor revenge. But now the time had come, the soul of one long dead, had lodged in an unknowing host. Slowly and surely, the evil soul would corrupt and control until —

"I am Tada, master of the mysteries
of Nin, seeker of In and Yo.
Know me now, for I am your master."

For a brief instant, the realisation of what he had done to himself, hit Tada's mortal soul. He drew his heavy-bladed tanto and set to thrust it into his stomach. But try as he might, he could not move his hand. In his ears, the sinister voice rang out.

"No, not yet. You and I have much work to do. I have waited these long years, a watcher in the shadows. Now is my time come again, and my vow is death to the Kuroda and all who oppose me."

The tanto fell uselessly to the ground as Tada, master of the ninja was completely possessed by the evil soul of his long-dead ancestor. But revenge and hate would have no death.

Cut deep!

The sealed box

CHAPTER TWELVE

the empty hand

"It is said that a blade of Muramasa, once drawn, will not be sheathed until it has tasted the warmth of life blood. Indeed was it not thus told by the great Toshogu, who when in life, was wounded by such a blade."

So saying, Kuroda Ichitaro unsheathed the heirloom of the Oka clan. It was a fine blade, strong in its curve and wild, fire wild in its forging. A man of great skill had beaten this into existence and in its creation, had imbued it with much of his own tortured madness. In the half light of the armoury, Kuroda lectured the

A Ronin – masterless Samurai – uses his sword to cook fish

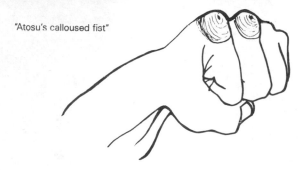
"Atosu's calloused fist"

Okinawan master, Atosu in the ways of the Samurai. He handed the fine blade to Atosu.

"Remember, don't touch the blade!"

Atosu held the blade carefully and looked at its perfect facets.

"I see that it is well made, but I'm sorry, I don't see the romance you Japanese put into it. With our weapons, they are used as weapons only when we are threatened. Otherwise, our Nunchaku is for flailing millet, our Tonfa for moving the grind stone and our Kama for harvesting."

Kuroda was about to reply immediately, but with the liberation that the Wind Spirit gave him; paused, thought for a moment and only then replied.

"You know Atosu, you have a point. True, the sword has no other use than as a weapon, save perhaps amongst the Ronin, who use it as a skewer to cook their chicken or fish. But this is to only look at it physically. Spiritually, the sword is beyond any such description. There is no utilitarian use for it, it is to feed the spirit and not the body."

"Hmm" replied Atosu, as he stroked the enormous callouses which protected his knuckles from the harshest onslaught. "That's not the way we see it on my island. There, the sword and your fine Samurai are just for one thing — keeping us down and

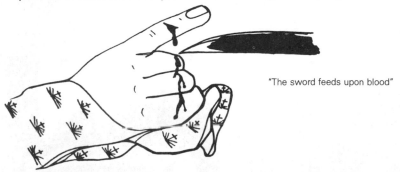
"The sword feeds upon blood"

"The remembrance candle burns
before the Kuroda altar"

The Kuroda heirloom

swaggering around. But there's many a Samurai who has regretted ridiculing the peasant and his humble rice flail. Make no mistake we are a peaceful race but" he clenched his mighty hand, the skin rasped as the knuckles cracked into their fighting mode, "we accept only so much."

Kuroda saw the natural dignity of this man and despite his own training in the role and place of Samurai, could not reply. Instead, he inclined his head slightly forward. In that instant, a link was forged between the two warriors. They remained in silence for a few minutes, the Muramasa blade glinted beckoningly; its super-hard edge pearly white.

"Tell me" said Atosu "all that about the blade being an evil one. Do you believe it?"

"Of course not" said Kuroda, who reached for the white wood resting scabbard. Carefully he sheathed the blade until only half an inch of edge was left exposed. Hoping that Atosu would not see, he placed his small finger of his left hand on the habaki guard and just slid it across the cutting edge. A tiny slash opened up, spreading a spot of blood. The blade here was corroded with "blood rust", as generations of guardians of the Oka armoury had done the same. Superstition it definitely was, but better to lose a spot of blood now, than swim in it later.

Atosu, all this time, seemed to be looking at the racks upon racks and rows upon rows of sword, spear and musket. But he had seen Kuroda's action. He found it strange, but as he had observed much that was alien in his dealings with Kuroda, he assigned it to his memory for another time.

Leaving Kuroda to his maintenance of the swords, Atosu walked down the fine wood walkway, polished glassy smooth with the feet of ten generations of Samurai. He saw, preserved with great honour, Sashimono battle standards from conflicts of four centuries previous. Turning a corner, he came to an area which was roped off with a purple silk hawser, tied with Shinto symbols in white paper. Paying this no heed, he hopped over and entered. There was little to see. Displayed on a white stand was a naginata halberd, a pair of swords, some scroll boxes and the Deity altar which contained the likeness of the first Kuroda and his wife, Shino.

The air became quiet, searching for a moment, the very crevices of Atosu's being, filling him with a calmness that only manifested itself after hours of rigorous training in the Kata form. Atosu's body suddenly felt light. He felt as though the entire world was his home — no discord, no desire, just all-encompassing calmness. A few moments later, he was aware that Kuroda had come up behind him. He turned and looked at Kuroda, who smiled and nodded his head slightly.

"Now you know."

"Yes", said Atosu, "I think that I do!"

"Good, it is as it should be. You are the first to understand the Kuroda Wind Spirit, who is not of direct descent from the master."

Atosu looked back at Kuroda, the veils were lifted and each understood the workings of the other's heart. Silently, they walked the corridors of the castle together. The bond of brotherhood that the Wind Spirit had bestowed upon them, made for true and deep understanding.

At long last, Kuroda knew that the time had come to speak, by this time they had reached the sand garden.

"Atosu, you must return to your homeland and I now pledge

that I will make this happen. I have but one simple request."

"Name it and it shall be yours."

"Show me your Okinawan way."

For a Samurai to even ask to be shown the Kobudo ways of Okinawa was a request always met with silence, but then, Kuroda was more than just any Samurai.

"Yes, I would like very much to show you a little of our way, for you have opened your house and heart to us. My only request is that none other in this whole world be party to this, for I break a vow of secrecy made to my masters back on my home island."

"You may depend upon me," promised Kuroda, "When do you suggest that we start?"

Atosu thought for a few moments.

"Four days hence at midnight, on the night with no moon – it is traditional with us. By the time of the three day moon, you will know the stances and by the full moon, you will know the breathing methods. By the time that there is again no moon, a man of your accomplishments, you will know all that I can show you."

This was indeed a great honour. In the space of the moon's waxing and waning, twenty eight days, Atosu would impart the secrets of a lifetime's study. The workings of the Wind Spirit were also set within him, on his return to Okinawa, he would synthesize a new and formidable system, the like of which had never been seen before – but that is another story.

The time is now midnight, on the night of no moon, in a field of rustling sasa grass on a moorland, a strong horse's ride from Oka Castle. The Samurai, Kuroda, faced the Okinawan, Atosu. Only the rustling of the breeze as it swayed and billowed the tall grass around them, bore witness to the "forging of spirit", as the

Okinawans term the deep practice of the mysteries.

From a distance away, it sounded as though some mighty tiger lurked in the verdant tangle, as the low growling Kiai that characterised the Okinawan form, manifested itself. Atosu was a patient but stern teacher. He had much to impart and his honour dictated that he must give his all to the task. For the ten thousandth time, his heavily calloused hand struck steel-hard and lightning-fast at Kuroda, first at his head, then at his chest and so on, throughout the long dark night. No words were spoken; just attack, attack. A fist, a foot, a flying kick, all were tough teachers and the lesson was learned, hard but true.

As the starlight gave way to the indigo of just before dawn, the two faced one another. Kuroda's face was swollen, both eyes were black, a stream of blood had mingled and then dried from both nose and mouth. His Kimono was in tatters as a result of Atosu's powerful throwing techniques, great red weals and purple/black bruising caused by Atosu's hands, feet, knees and elbows and head, showed through the ripped garment. Kuroda smiled. He looked like a demon in this weird light.

"Tomorrow night" said Atosu. Kuroda bowed,

"Now it is my time, here a bargain is struck," he paused to spit out a tooth then continued, "we will go to the library. Anything which you wish to see, you may.

Atosu thought,

"No, not today, I have neglected my men for long enough. They need to know their fate. I will return to this place tomorrow night at the same time."

True to his word, on the next night and the next, the relentless training went on. Almost imperceptibly, Kuroda was actually

Nagemaki

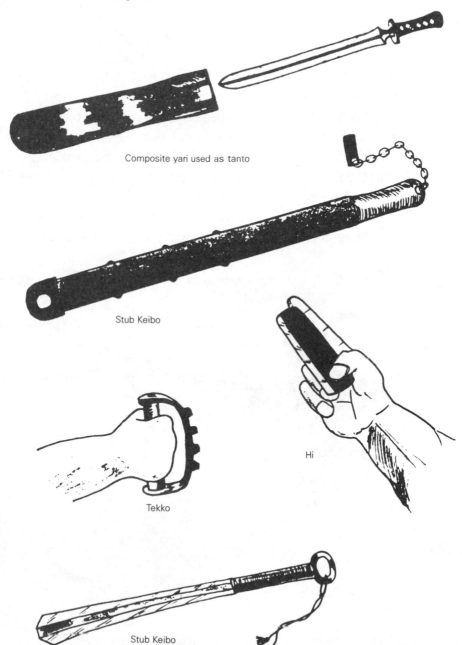

Composite yari used as tanto

Stub Keibo

Tekko

Hi

Stub Keibo

receiving fewer and fewer blows. Full face strikes now met with steel-hard blocks or with an evasion, soft as a maiden's cheek. It is truly said, in fencing, that a poor student receives heavy blows; so too in this alien form, the increase in skill became the saviour of the body. So it continued, until, as Atosu had predicted by the light of the three day moon, Kuroda had mastered the physical.

Atosu launched a back kick to Kuroda's kidneys. Kuroda caught its spirit, turned in the swiftly spinning arc and blocked Atosu's outstretched foot, first with his knee and then with a

"All over the city the Ninja wait for the call to arms"

cupped hand. He parried deftly and the blow that could sunder a tree trunk fell as ripe fruit.

"Good" said Atosu, speaking for the first time during their training sessions.

"But the moon is yet young, you have much to learn. I have it in mind, that by the time of no moon, we will perform true Kumite battle — you with your sword and me with my Kama and Hari No Sai."

Kuroda nodded. It would be an apt graduation, Kuroda knew that the fight would indeed be a real one. Only the dawn light would signal a stop, unless his training had been lax and death ended it first — but that was as yet, many days in the future.

"Fight today's battle today and tomorrow's battle tomorrow, for tomorrow never comes" as the sword master, Otani, would have it.

Whilst this grassland academy was in session in far away Dewa Province, a sinister force moved in the land. The ninja master, Tada, possessed by the spirit of the long dead, plotted an evil end to the House of Kuroda. On the second anniversary of the devastation of the forts on Choshu by the Dutch, French and

British, 1866, revenge was set in motion. A man is the summary of his memories. the pain of Japan's wounding bit deeply into the heart of every man and woman who held true the spirit of Japan. Never mind what the lofty talkers of Edo and Osaka would say — the true feeling of those who proudly bore the sword felt the wound and bore the scar for generations to come. In such an environment, those who did not fear the policies of what passed for a government, waited for the moment.

All across the country, the tools and toys of the barbarians were filling the once clean rooms of the Japanese. As had happened a generation before — heads cut cleanly from their bodies, were displayed in the streets. No barbarian was safe from the onslaught of the patriots who called themselves, Shi Shi. The ninja master Tada infiltrated into this land of warriors and unrest. By "calling in a few debts" he gained swift ascendancy through their ranks. With his tactics, the haphazard "kill anything with round eyes" policy was replaced by a definite "hit list". When Tada felt that he was in a strong enough position he awoke the 'sleeping tigers' and called together the new ninja of Tomokatsu Ryu. For some strange reason, he called their meeting on a beach, a fair

The Samurai and the Okinawan-brothers in Budo

distance from Edo. By black of night they assembled, just as their ancestors had done, over two centuries before.

Songoro the dwarf, slid between the ranks of the ninja until he took up position at the front of the throng.

"Brothers and sisters" said Tada, "Long have you slept, now awake and unsheath your swords; blood will flow."

Songoro looked at the face of his master Tada, lit by a flickering fire-brand. In the distance, the waves crashed against the jagged rocks. Something was wrong. Songoro could not put a name to it, but his master did not seem the same. Somehow, he seemed harder, distant, there was an icy edge to his spirit. Songoro pondered these things as he listened to Tada, but what to do about it?

Tada's voice swelled to fever pitch as he shouted out the plans for action. All the legations were to be infiltrated, all personal maids, courtesans and servants of the foreigners were to be replaced by ninja and on one tumultuous night, all were to be murdered. "The night of cold steel", as Tada named it, would be heralded by the ringing of the great bell in the precincts of the French Legation in Edo. With a concerted effort, the Shi Shi would rise up and replace the Shōgun. The port at the Yokohama would be burnt to the ground, along with the areas at Osaka and Nagasaki. In one night, the calendar would be turned back two hundred years. But before that, Tada had the little matter of some personal business – in Dewa Province.

Okinawan Kon fighting stance

the heavens awake

On the night of no moon, under a star-filled sky, a sword was unsheathed. In a furious attack, it met the metal of a Kama sickle and Hari no Sai. Blades sparked as the forces of two strong warriors attacked and parried. The grass bore witness to this duel of Titans, as with all the skill of twenty generations of men proud to bear the title, Samurai, the razor edge of the sword cut and thrust. Hot breath panted and sweat poured this night of nights away. The forces of the Wind Spirit watched dispassionately — victory to the stronger. So the duel progressed, minutes ticked into hours as the night passed. Then, with the dawn light reflecting dully on sword and sickle, the two warriors drew apart, a good distance separated them. At a precise moment, both sword and sickle were set aside. Unarmed, save for their spirits, the two men faced each other. Tears of joy broke out on both faces at the realisation that the test was over. Both had emerged victorious, the seal of the Wind Spirit was set upon both of them and never again would they turn a weapon upon one another. It was as though the two were one, both shared the same profound experience that is the core of the warrior's heart.

"You know," began Atosu, "when I return to the Ryu Kyu, I shall never be the same man who left. This depth that the Wind Spirit has allowed me to glimpse, sets me apart."

A ninja studies the new way

"Yes" said Kuroda "and the insight into the Te that you have given me, marks me apart from the rest of my countrymen. You know, we are souls who are lost in space, but perhaps this is fortunate, for I believe that the next few years will see such a disruption of the old life that we will not recognise ourselves."

"Then" said Atosu "it is time for me and mine to return to Ryu Kyu."

"Aye!" said Kuroda, "best be well out of it. I know that I shall retire from public life and pursue my arts alone. I intend to take to the mountains, live in a two-mat hut; my sword and spear as my companions. I have a mind to develop a form mentioned in the Ura scroll, its basic name is Yari No Tsuki, the Moon Spear, I feel that its rudiments have great potential."

Atosu gazed into the middle distance, the sun cut the horizon. He longed, now that his task was completed, to return home. Kuroda stopped in mid-sentence,

"Excuse me, how unforgiveable, I have neglected my part of the bargain. We will make all necessary arrangements. I swear

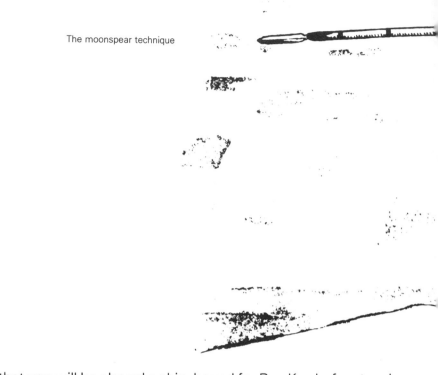

The moonspear technique

that you will be aboard a ship, bound for Ryu Kyu before ten days have slipped into eleven."

True to his word, upon their return to the grounds of Oka Castle, a messenger was sent to a harbour in the north of the province. His letters of leave said that the voyage was to Sado Island, but the extra provisions that were secretly bought, told a different story.

The last days passed swiftly in a round of quiet gatherings. The Okinawans readied themselves, each tied on the single ingot of gold "liberated" from the blockhouse so long ago. The gold would be their passport to wealth back on the islands.

Amidst all these preparations, Kuroda felt a vague, nameless unease, as though a heavy blanket was laid upon his shoulders. On the eve of the Okinawans' departure, Atosu confronted Kuroda on the yard-wide granite steps leading to the Keep. With

characteristic bluntness he looked Kuroda in the eyes, his steely gaze penetrated deep.

"Something is wrong for you, I know, I feel it."

"Yes, my friend, I have a feeling of foreboding, something evil, powerfully evil is stretching out to grasp me."

"How long have you felt it?"

"Oh, about three days now."

"And each day it grows a little stronger?" asked Atosu.

"Yes" said Kuroda "somehow I know that its intent is for me, and me alone."

"Come with us to Ryu Kyu then, let's put some sea between it and you."

"No" said Kuroda, "I have a feeling that I know what it is. I must check the hall of records, one of my forefathers had a similar experience, or so the legend goes. But his secret diary is in the record hall, if anything can help it will be that. Come with me Atosu, you are like a brother, this should be for your eyes also."

With that, Kuroda turned and walked down the steps. He walked past an open space which bore a memorial to Kuroda Ichitaro who had caught the full force of a fusillade of musket fire, past the graves of Kuroda Ichitaro and Shino, his wife, and into the

stone built hall of records.

A Samurai guard leapt to attention as he saw Kuroda and Atosu appear. The tip of his yari spear quivered as he strove to stand at attention.

"Relax your shoulders" said Kuroda. "Never use a spear with hard shoulders."

The guard's face reddened slightly and he relaxed his shoulders. Kuroda swept past. Drawing his long sword scabbard out, he placed it upon a well-worn rack. The interior of the great hall was dark, save for flickering candles, placed at odd intervals to penetrate the blueness.

There came a rustling in the mid-distance as the keeper of the records hall, came out to see what was happening, on seeing Kuroda, his eyes beamed.

"Ah master! Welcome, welcome."

He saw the menacing bulk of Atosu for the first time.

"And your friend" he quickly added, "what can I do to be of assistance?"

"Well," said Kuroda, "about two hundred years ago; a journal by a Kuroda of that time."

"Hmm, let me see," he drew out a fan, he flicked it open to reveal the keeper's filing system.

"Ah, yes, here we have it, aisle six, come, come."

He scurried off. Kuroda and Atosu followed, finally they all drew up by a long low table.

"Be seated, gentlemen. I have the box here."

He lifted the dusty laquer lid of the box which contained the journal, a smell of great age exuded.

"Thank you, you may leave us now."

The keeper bowed and scuttled off. Seated together, Kuroda and Atosu scanned the long journal. They read of many adventures against ninja. Of the intervention by spirits and of a final battle where the first Tada had been killed. Kuroda put the scroll down on the table.

"Hmm, I think I know now."

Atosu, catlike, sniffed the air, "something burns." Kuroda made to fold the journal scroll up for safety, but as his fingers reached for it, the elegant Kanji characters glowed red and then burst into flame, Kuroda leapt back.

"Back to back!" shouted Atosu.

Back to back, they both probed the darkness. The smell of burning had gone now. Atosu scanned the half of darkness that was his. One by one, the candles flickered blue and were extinguished leaving them in total blackness.

"The door!" said Kuroda and crablike, they edged toward it, allowing no gap or break in their defences. In a dark corner, a faint green glow began to pulsate, slowly at first, then faster and faster. The orb of light started to grow arms, then legs, the eerie green suffused all around it with a deathly pallor, as there stood before them a Samurai, clad in the battle armour of six centuries before. He was gigantic, well over eight feet tall, his long hair reached his waist. His face had the same green colour, but his eyes — his eyes dripped blood, red and wet. Kuroda drew his short sword blade, carved into it was the image of Fudo No Myo — the immovable. The blade, thrice blessed in the forging and thrice blessed in the sharpening, glowed white and pure.

"By this sacred blade, I swear my truth. Step forward and fight, or be gone to whatever hole spawned thee!"

Training with the iron bound bokken

Ninja wall sealer "Nekotobi"

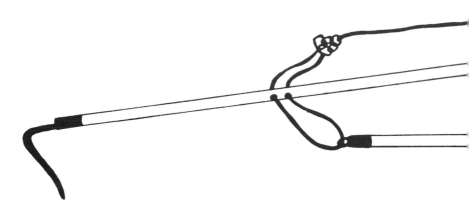

The green Samurai opened his cavernous mouth, a torrent of blood and gore issued forth, with the rasping words — "I come for you, come for you." It moved forward, drawing its huge sword, taller than a man.

Atosu leaped forward in a high kick that would have sundered the very pillars of Ise. But his kick never hit home, for as it targetted, Atosu chanted his own words of self-protection and the entity dissolved away. Atosu's good heart, in self sacrifice, had protected him and driven the entity back to whatever hell it had come from. As it disappeared, the candles came alight again and Kuroda rushed over to help Atosu to his feet.

"You saved my life."

"Nah!" said Atosu, "I just couldn't resist having a crack at a Samurai that big!"

Modestly, Atosu patted the dust from his clothes. With an iron clang, the doors opened and the keeper scurried in —

"Masters, you need something?"

"Yes" said Kuroda, pointing to the burned scroll, "an accident."

"Oh!" was all the keeper could say as he pattered over to see what could be salvaged.

"Come Atosu, I must speak with you." They left the hall of

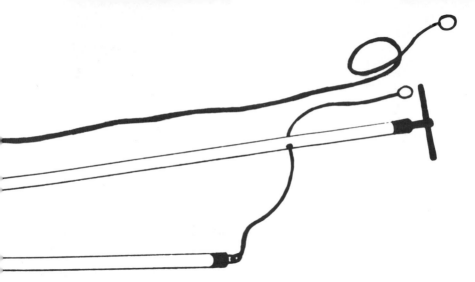

records, Kuroda led him to the mausoleum which held both Kuroda Ichitaro and Shino. He picked a bundle of green incense from a camphor wood box. With a taper kept for the purpose, he lit the incense, the ends glowed red. Kuroda blew across it and a trail of blue, grey pine fragrance spiralled heavenward. Kuroda placed them carefully at the foot of the graves and clapped his hands together. He silently prayed for guidance, then turning to Atosu, he began to speak.

"The spell missed its target that time. Whoever is sending it, will be weakened for a while."

"I say let's hunt him down and crack his skull like an egg" interrupted Atosu.

"No! Atosu my brother, I asked you to be a party to the scroll, but I will not ask you to be a party to this. Your's is another destiny. Mine is solitary."

"What do you propose to do?"

"My old teacher always said, 'when in doubt step forward'. I"ll take his advice. The malignant force is weaker, whilst it rests I will trace it to its heart."

"I'll not make any fuss" said Atosu, "I know you too well to try and divert you from your task. So I will bid you farewell now. Life is a strange mystery indeed."

With that, Atosu turned. He walked to the compound where the rest of his party waited. Within the hour, they had left, never

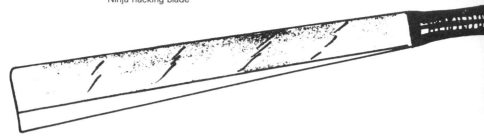

ones to mince words; true hearts indeed, but a goodbye was a goodbye.

Selecting a horse, more for stamina than for speed, Kuroda bid farewell to Oka Castle, the trustee-ship was passed into capable hands. Adjusting his travelling jingasa helmet, Kuroda spurred his horse headlong down the path of the evil force. As each crossroads came and went, Kuroda felt the evil's strength increasing. He was close now to the raw nerve of revenge.

After four day's non-stop travel, his horse gave up the struggle and dropped like a stone, dead. Kuroda turned left then right, like a needle the edge of pain jarred his flesh. The force was close. He looked up to an almost sheer rock face. Intertwining up it was a series of avalanche stops and rocky outcrops. Using these as a makeshift stairway, he scaled the precipice. As his fingers grasped the clear air at the top of his climb, the atmosphere boiled with pent-up evil.

"Steadily onward!" Kuroda quietly said to himself. He breached the top of the precipice and surveyed the flat table-like expanse of rock which stretched out before him – nothing. Then he rubbed his eyes. He saw a twisted, gnarled figure, a cruel caricature of what it had once been. With bent arthritic fingers, a hand beckoned to Kuroda.

"Come here" croaked a cracked voice,
"I have been expecting you.
I am Tada."

the night of cold steel

All across Japan, the New Ninja awaited the signal for action. Infiltrated into all the foreigner's legations and at the dock at the Yokohama; they awaited their master's call to arms, signalled by the ringing of the old temple bell in the compound of the French legation. Using the barbarians' talking wire, the message would be telegraphed down the line and barbarian blood would once and for all spill across the defiled tatami in the haunts of the foreign scum, all over Dai Nihon.

But before they could strike, the bell had first to be rung and at the moment, their leader had other dealings. Cracked and wizened with premature age brought on by the return of the evil one, Tada's eyes shone fish-like, dull and half-glazed, moved by an independent force. The evil force which had guided Kuroda to him, had somewhat sapped his energy. Kuroda saw him, crouched over a smoking pile of embers. He knotted and unknotted his fingers in the mudra patterns of the Kankuji mind control as he desperately tried to regain his strength. He did not notice that Kuroda had circled round behind him, sword hilt and scabbard readied. So, this pathetic creature was Tada, master of the Tomokatsu Ryu Ninja, inheritor of the deep, dark ways. Kuroda almost felt pity, but pity only goes so far. As he drew within striking distance, he twisted the scabbard of his long sword so that the edge faced down, he prepared to cut Kesa Giri. His right hand reached for the blue silk itomaki binding, his fingers closed on the handle and began to slowly draw the sword out, silently it travelled towards its target.

Although Tada's spiritual powers were depleted, his animal nature and will to survive were just as strong. As the sword blade scythed upwards, to double cut Kesa Giri, the old ninja way took

over and a pellet of blinding powder was thrown at Kuroda. He switched his cut to a Hasso deflection and the pellet exploded with a puff of yellow dust, well off target. But some of the wind-borne dust attacked Kuroda's eyes and for a few vital seconds, they streamed tears. When he regained his full sight, Tada was gone. He heard a clatter of small rocks coming from the edge of the precipice. He looked over, about six feet down, on a rocky ledge, Tada had firmly tied a stout hemp rope, it was down this that he was making good his escape. Kuroda leaped down the six feet, landing lightly on the moss covered rocks, with his short sword he hacked through the taut rope. One cut, the rope twanged as the tension in it was released and it dropped over the edge. "Too late, damn it." Tada was only ten feet from the ground, he dropped smoothly, cat-like. As Kuroda watched helplessly, he scampered to his horse. He noticed a strange thing — Tada was straighter, taller — the forces of regeneration were working their mystery. Kuroda realised that he had no time to lose, he must follow wherever Tada led, before enough power had been generated for Tada to send another nameless demon against him. Steeling himself, Kuroda made the quickest descent he knew how, bouncing and sliding down the rocky scree.

He looked at the tracks at the bottom of the precipice and

By sword and nata

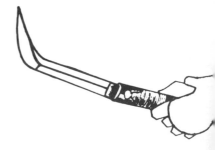

Kuroda realised that there was only one place that Tada could go, Edo. With this in mind, he hitched up his hakama and began to run. His speed was constant, and within two hours, he saw a way station. A silver coin passed, and Kuroda had a horse again. He spurred the animal on by pressing the rough iron abumi stirrups hard into the horse's flanks. After an eternity of hot pursuit, the dust of Tada was in the air. Through border posts, jumping barriers, over spearmen, they sped. Tada was able to look back, his face, although dust marked, was young again, his eyes burned

with a demon fire. Kuroda realised that whilst he was being pursued, Tada could not invoke the ceremonies to release demons. He must not fail – onward faster. Stretch the sinews and exert the spirit.

"Tada, I shall see you dead!" he shouted to spur himself on, but his words were not heard by Tada, the wind carried them away with the dust.

But Tada, fully aware of his pursuer, had an appointment – just a matter of ringing a bell in the compound of the French Legation. His vow of death to Kuroda would have to wait. Down half-made roads he sped, until in the distance, hazed blue with the smoke from ten thousand hibachi braziers, lay the majesty that was Edo, capital of the Shōgun. Just before he neared the Sumida barrage, Tada executed a flip kick. Using one stirrup as a jumping off point, he side-jumped and allowed the horse to gallop on, spreading a cloud of fine dust. In the shade of a cedar tree, he deftly changed into normal clothes, carried in his loin cloth. In this fashion, he set off down the left bank of the Sumida, until he encountered a ferryman. His boat was old and leaked a little, he baled it out every so often with a cone of wax paper.

"Good day sire" said the ferryman with mock respect, "off to Yoshiwara then?" (Yoshiwara, the forbidden. Palace to a thousand delights.)

The ferryman grinned a gap-toothed smile, his oily face creasing like old leather. Then he looked at Tada's face, at his eyes – he shut up! Tada boarded the ricketty wooden boat. It rocked from side to side as though the water spirit would have no part of this evil. But Tada was unmoved he sat down.

"Row!" he said. The ferryman, who sincerely wished that he

Ninja combat

The French legation bell

was somewhere else, grasped the single oar in his scrawny arms. It seemed to the ferryman that the voyage had lasted a year, but in reality, it was less than sixty paces then the boat bumped against the wooden piles sunk into the far bank. Tada jumped up and out of the boat, throwing a coin behind him. The ferryman left the coin where it landed. Instead he struck out with the great oar with all his might in an effort to put as much space as possible between himself and Tada.

Tada was gone like a shadow, melting into the bright lights and mock gaiety of the Yoshiwara. It was a smart move, Kuroda would have great trouble finding him in all this bustle. As he walked determinedly, he dodged down side alleys where the Oiran prostitutes, who had survived to an age where a house would not want them, plied their lonely trade. One or two of them accosted Tada, but as he glided past, they soon realised their mistake and turned their attentions instead to the barbarian sailors weaving drunkenly about in the darkness. As Tada checked and re-checked his escape, he came up against many of the foreign devils, tall and smelling of boiled pork and perfume. Tada's earthly nature revelled in the fact that his would be the hand to signal the bloody end of all this barbarian filth. Then his spirit ruler again took over, forbidding such pleasure. First, the task in hand must be completed, then sweet, final revenge; the death vows of the centuries, fulfilled in the space of a night.

Speeding headlong in the wake of Tada's dust, Kuroda spurred the wilting horse onwards. Soon the Tokkaido was crossed and the Nihon Bashi stretched out in front like a gently curving hill. Kuroda suddenly drew his horse up, the horse slithered. Kuroda leaped off, his Kimono and hakama red/grey

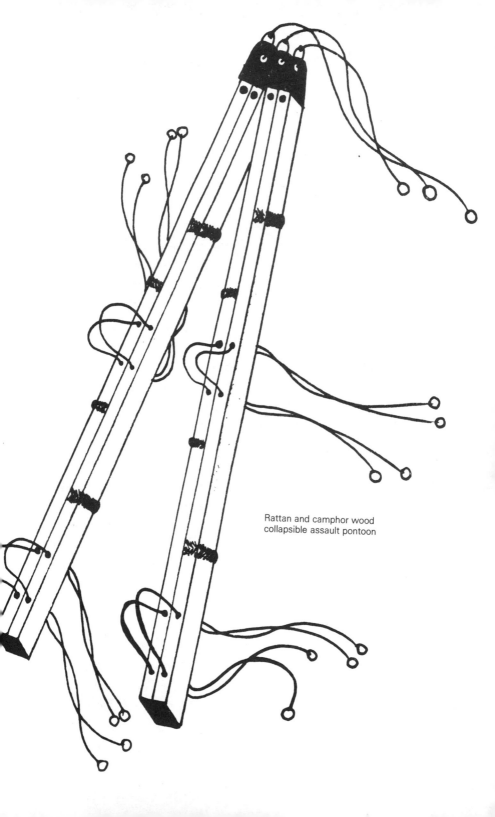

Rattan and camphor wood
collapsible assault pontoon

with road dust. Something was amiss. The road led on, the tracks of Tada's horse carried onward but the spirit was missing. Kuroda quietened his breathing and waited for the Wind Spirit to manifest itself. A timeless moment passed. A great calmness drifted over Kuroda, the noise and clamour of the Shōgun's capital faded into a dull buzz, the smell of the bonfire by which the bridge watch warmed themselves faded to a distant vague scent. Through his half-closed eyes, the living present that men called real time, faded away – the Wind Spirit called all to its bosom and in loving reconciliation, cradled them. Those who were its chosen had no fear and no longing. In a multitude of emotions and visions, Kuroda saw his spirit brother, Atosu. He heard the roar of the sea and the crack of sail cloth as the wind drove the ship onwards. Then the scene shifted and all was madness – lights and noise. Turning and twisting snatches of a thousand different tunes played on demon instruments, rocked through his head. Then the image of a bell, then a sword, then a veritable river of blood gushing down stone steps. Then blackness. Kuroda's mind restored itself to the real time, his left eye twitched in rhythm with his heartbeat as consciousness returned to him. With a supreme quelling of old emotions, Kuroda calmed himself, sometimes the deep gaze revealed only what may be, not necessarily what will be. Before him, the road was clear, and he strode off along it without hesitating. Looking straight ahead, he walked to the banks of the Sumida, to the very same boatman. By the expression on the boatman's face, Kuroda could see that Tada had been this way. Without so much as a murmur, the boatman ferried Kuroda across the river, soon the pleasure grounds of the Yoshiwara were in sight.

"The Shi-Shi arise! To cut down a foreigner"

Kuroda strode purposefully on. Russian sailors, fully half a body bigger than him, stepped aside as they felt the spirit of real Budo. In the haunts of Oiran, a few cut-purses lurked, to their greedy eyes Kuroda's classical dress marked him out as a country bumpkin up for a fling. As Kuroda caught the scent like a hunting dog, he whirled around a corner into a dark alley way; without a pause he went deeply into it. Suddenly he was aware that he was not alone. Two men had slipped out of the side doorways where the sweet smell of Chinese opium drifted like a sickly, cloying demon spider. In front of Kuroda, another two stepped out, blocking his way. One of the men held an extremely long Hocho kitchen cleaver, he grinned with a mouth that had lost most of its teeth.

"Give us your money!" he said.

"Ay, and his sword" shouted another voice.

"Yeah, and his clothes, they're good silk" put in another.

Kuroda slowed down to a steady walk, at no time did he step backwards.

"So, you want my money?" Without waiting for an answer he continued

"and my sword?"

One of the men behind him did a very stupid thing, he made to strike at Kuroda's head. As his arm raised up, Kuroda side stepped and the wooden club met thin air. Kuroda's sword leapt from its scabbard and cut off the man's thumb, without pause, it continued and cut both insteps. The man dropped, alive, but useless. The thug bearing the hocho, made to slash across at Kuroda's eye height. In a double reverse, the blade cut the juncture between hand and wrist, as the ligament was severed, the hand involuntarily sprang open, the hocho fell to the ground. Before it hit the

ground Kuroda's sword butt had struck the man cleanly on the chin, his jaw gently dislocated, leaving him gasping for air.

"Want some more?" Kuroda growled as the remaining two wondered exactly what they could do. Their eyes popped wide at the sight of such speed.

"Get him!" screamed the one without a thumb.

But to no avail, the remaining pair were showing a clean pair of heels as they hastened to put a great deal of space between themselves and this Samurai of the old school. Disgusted by their lack of fighting spirit, Kuroda continued on his pre-destined way. Carefully and quietly he cleaned and re-sheathed his sword as he walked.

Past Oiran houses, the way led. Through the silk dyers' warehouses, where the smell of dye filled the air. The feeling of unease became stronger as the foreigners' area drew nearer. Kuroda felt how strange for such an area to have no guards, but not really, for all awaited Tada's call to arms. Kuroda walked unopposed, down made-up roads flanked with cut stone walls, topped with the flags of the foreign nations. The presence was now overpowering. The temperature began to drop, an icy coldness pervaded the air. Kuroda invoked the deeper recesses of his art. Near a wall which sported the red, white and blue stripes of the French republic, Kuroda stopped almost as though a glass wall forbade him further progress. He sought the depth. Tada, ninja master, was gaining in strength, but he was not back to his full power yet, for he could only manage the coldness. He could not yet conjure up one of the elementals which had almost destroyed him in the hall of records.

Kuroda walked unchallenged into the compound. Lights were low and not a sound could be heard. With a start, Kuroda saw in one corner, the bell which he had glimpsed in his vision. Seated at its base was Tada, again invoking the ninja deities. Kuroda drew his sword and in the manner of his forebears, threw the scabbard away — this battle would be the final conflict. The vow of two centuries would be fulfilled, or in failure, Kuroda would die a Samurai's death.

Inner secrets of the warrior's heart

Tanto grips

With a slight air of annoyance Tada broke off his ritual. He turned and saw Kuroda. As he rose from the squatting position, the civilian clothes fell away to reveal red/black ninja combat fatigues. Tada merged into the shadows, except for his eyes, which burned blood red. Part of Tada's brain told him that he must give the signal for the night of cold steel, but in the depths of demon possession, the undead worked its will, Tada was now completely its slave.

"No living hand shall kill me" Tada said.

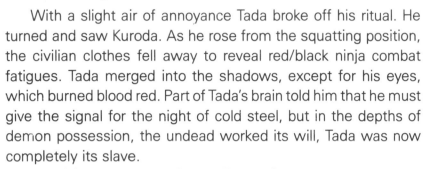

The handle of a ninja dagger

He leaped forward out of the shadows. His musori blade flickered. Battle was joined. The techniques of Wind Spirit parried and struck. Kuroda used many of Atosu's techniques, but punches and kicks had no effect upon Tada's body, possessed as it was by he who was better still dead. Sparks flew as blade encountered blade, and blade hit stone. With one final effort, Kuroda cut Kesa Giri. But Tada was master of his art and the finely executed cut missed. The ninja musori blade cut back and Kuroda's right arm fell uselessly down. It still held his sword, a rush of arterial blood sprayed out onto the flagstones. Kuroda's body sagged forward and he slumped to his knees. Frantically he sought the inner strength that was the heart of the Wind Spirit. Tada cried in triumph as flecks of Kuroda's blood spattered his face, his sword snaked upwards to take Kuroda's head, then stopped.

"No — first the sign, destroy all
barbarian filth. Then slow death by a
thousand cuts, my little Samurai."

Tada spat the words out with a demon croak. Vile laughter filled the air.

Tada then turned and made for the bell. He grasped the great oak clapper and began to swing it. Slowly it swang at the great bronze bell. Nearer, nearer, a thousand would die at the sound of its echo. Kuroda's head was racked with pain. The deep strength that was the Wind Spirit had deserted him. Then in the courtyard of the French Legation, a gentle wind began to blow. With the combined strength of those who bore the name Kuroda, Kuroda Ichitaro opened his eyes. With his left arm, he picked up his severed right arm which still held his sword. With a final cry Kuroda threw his arm, sword and all through the air. Faster and truer than a heron's flight, the sword sped. It pierced Tada's back and came out through his chest, impaling him to the great oak clapper. The force of the strike pushed it away from the bell. Tada whirled around and with the clapper in tow, fell in a disarranged heap at the bottom of two stone steps. He looked wildly about, trying to reach the bell.

"Why? How?" Tada asked through a veil of blood.

Fighting through the mists of his own pain, Kuroda spoke with the strength of the true warrior.

"Tada, you said that no living hand could kill you!"

The elementals let go their grasp and a dull green glow filled Tada's face, he exploded with green fire which consumed his earthly body.

Kuroda looked on, the pain in his shoulder had subsided a little. He stood up, the smoking body of Tada, master of the Tomokatsu Ryu Ninja and host to demons, had paid the price. With his left hand, he picked his sword from out of the ashes, strangely it was cool, untouched by the green inferno.

The night of cold steel had been averted and the sleeping tigers of Tomokatsu Ryu slept on for a little longer, awaiting he who would awaken them.

Kuroda found his scabbard and walked off into a future that would have little use for a swordsman, let alone a one-armed Samurai.

"Kuroda — the one armed
Samurai walks away"

**"BEHOLD, THE ICE,
COLD AS MY VOW OF DEATH!"**
(from the secret scrolls of the Tomokatsu Ryu)

Other Titles published by Dragon Books

Nunchaku Dynamic Training
By Hirokazu Kanazawa 8th Dan **$9.95**

Advanced Shotokan Kata Series
By Keinosuke Enoeda 8th Dan

Volume 1
Bassai-Dai : Kanku-Dai : Jion : Empi : Hangetsu **$14.95**

Volume 2
Bassai-Sho : Kanku-Sho : Jiin : Gankaku : Sochin **$14.95**

Volume 3
Tekki-Nidan : Tekki-Sandan *(2 versions)* : Nijushiho
: Gojushiho-Dai : Gojushiho-Sho **$14.95**

Dynamic Kicking Method
By Masafumi Shiomitsu 7th Dan **$9.95**

Shadow of the Ninja
By Katsumi Toda **$7.95**

Revenge of the Shogun's Ninja
By Katsumi Toda **$7.95**

Kubotan Keychain – Instrument of Attitude Adjustment
By Takayuki Kubota 8th Dan **$7.95**

The Ninja Star – Art of Shuriken Jutsu
By Katsumi Toda **$6.95**

Balisong – Iron Butterfly
By Cacoy Hernandez **$7.95**

When the Going Gets Tough
By Col. M. Smythe (in preparation) **$7.95**

Naked Blade – A Manual of Japanese Swordsmanship
By Toshishiro Obata 8th Dan **$8.95**

Close Encounters – The Arresting Art of Taiho-Jutsu
By Takayuki Kubota 8th Dan (in preparation) **$8.95**

The Ninja Sword – Art of Silent Kenjutsu
By Katsumi Toda **$7.95**

——————— Forthcoming Titles ———————
The Ninja Sword – Art of Silent Kenjutsu by Katsumi Toda
Close Encounters – The Arresting Art of Taiho Jutsu by Takayuki Kubota
Kama – The Art of the Infinite Circle by Toshishiro Obata

Dragon Books are available from branches of B. Dalton Booksellers, Walden Books and all good martial arts and general bookstores. If you have difficulty obtaining any of these titles, please contact the publisher direct. Orders under $10 can be filled for the advertised price plus $1.50. For orders over $10 simply add 10% to the value of your order to cover freight and handling charges. Overseas customers, please contact us for details of export shipping costs.

Dragon Books P.O. Box 6039 Thousand Oaks CA 91359 USA

Phototypeset in the United Kingdom by Concise Graphics Ltd. Hammersmith London